Midnight Simmer Tree

By RH Carroll

Foreword:

I miss midnight snacks.

That's how this collection of short stories, random thoughts, essays, unsent letters, poems, and miscellanea came into being. It is true, I do miss midnight snacks a great deal. In attempting to redefine my relationship with food, I needed to redirect that energy in a more positive direction. So, I began writing. I had never figured on becoming a writer. I was going to be an illustrator, but a disastrous foray into art school and all of that world's ugliness made that impossible.

But that is another story.

Looking back, I've written my whole life. Simply put, I never took it seriously. It was just something I played with to pass time or to privately vent difficult emotions.

This collection has undergone a few title changes. I've settled on Midnight Simmer Tree. It refers to my ongoing struggles with insomnia, to my approaching the midway point in my lifespan and observing a strange symmetry, to a play on words wherein I comment on the mysterious pressure and slow bubbling of emotions just under the surface, and to all the stages of life that can be symbolically expressed in the passing seasons and their effect on a tree. Midnight Simmer Tree. It's not especially clever, but it is the best title I came up with for my first foray into writing.

As I write more and begin to mature a very small amount as a writer, I see how much Samuel Clemens and Charles Dickens have influenced me. I hope that they would be at least mildly amused at my amateurish attempt to steal from them.

Forgive my pretentiousness and self-indulgence. I hope to not seem pedantic or lost in navel gazing. Honestly, I simply wish to share a sense of hope with people.

I hope you enjoy reading this as much as I enjoyed writing it.

Acknowledgements:

Most books have acknowledgments and thank you's up front. At least I clearly remember, as a kid, all the really good ones did. To those who were most directly inspirational in the creation of this work, here are mine.

In no particular order: Tony Ochoa, T. Williams, Christopher "Ogre" Wyatt, Robert R. Smetek, Denise Hill, "Debbie Izzaguirre", Ronald Owens, Don Longo Jr., Michael Hendrix, Joshua Starnes, Julai Whipple, Kelly Drath, The Harrigan Family, Lynell Ingram, Todd Wescott, Jamie Mallory, Shawn Johnson, Shelby Carter, Taylore Kyle, Kriestienn D., Zachary Rieck, Prof. Ken Jones, and April Martinez. For showing me the way, for accepting me as I am, for your enthusiasm, for your faith in me even in small things, for your honesty, for being an excellent wingman, for sticking up for me, for inspiring me, for your kindness in helping me hang on longer than I would've been able to otherwise, and for being the faithful keeper of my trust. You may have thought that you were doing some small simple kindness, but it meant the world to me. Check all that apply and take as many as you like. ;)

There are many more good friends and lovely acquaintances whose companionship and camaraderie were greatly appreciated and carried me when the times were... *sub-optimal*. Sincere and heartfelt thanks to all of you.

I would also like to thank Michael W. Kaluta for his encouragement and advice. Thanks also to Tony and Angela DiTerlizzi for being so very cool to me. Additionally, I would like to thank Stan "The Man" Lee for the best advice that took me nearly twenty-five years to fully take hold of: "*Never give up on your dreams, kid.*"

Most of all: Mom, you believed that I could accomplish anything, even when I didn't. Jeff, you will always be my favorite super hero, big brother.

Chapter One:

Bea Arthur and the Lost Temple of the Naga

Bea and I began this expedition into the Tibetan Himalayas in the spring of 1983 with a Sherpa guide we knew only as Thursday. It was three days into the mountains and our Sherpa, a superstitious fellow, had abandoned us in the night. Bea had gone off earlier that day to find some food. And I started to feel panic creep in as the hours passed. She had instructed me to, under no circumstances, leave the tent. A rushing fear I had never experienced before took over and before I could grab hold of myself, I was outside, ankle deep in show. I did not know how far, or in what direction I had ran. I could not see the camp any more.

I cried out, hoping that someone, anyone was in earshot. It was in vain. Who could possibly be here, out beyond the edge of human civilization? Visibility was hampered by the snow which came down in angry sheets. The wind was an icy lash that haphazardly sliced into anything foolish enough to attempt to defy it. I chose a direction and stumbled forward. After five shaky steps, it felt as if the ground gave out beneath me and I tumbled head over foot down the mountain. I stopped abruptly having mercifully landed in a snow bank. It sank in that now I was truly lost. Just as that thought crystallized in my mind, I heard a deep, low, guttural growl.

I rolled over and looked up slowly. My heart was pounding in my ears. What was before me was impossible. It stood up and blotted out the sky. This huge, hairy bestial thing locked eyes with me. It was bipedal and ape-like. But unlike an ape, it stood erect. It was brilliantly white with thick fur and a shaggy mane. Its eyes were fiercely blue and held a terrible predatory gaze. Its teeth were exposed in a horrific display of aggression. The smell was like putrefying meat. I was frozen in fear. I remember a strange laugh at the deep absurdity of this death began to bubble up.

In the instant before the creature was going to pounce, something flew into its face. The beast let out an incredible bellowing roar that left my ears ringing. Its eyes settled on something just behind me and to my left. What had been hurled was the limp body of a young mountain goat. I quickly turned my head to look behind me and saw Bea, long gleaming Bowie knife in hand, in readied posture, speaking in a calm but confident tone to the monster. Her steely gaze was locked onto it. "Easy now, big fella. You've got a free meal. No need to make this uglier than it has to be." There seemed to be the vaguest twinkling of understanding in the creature's countenance. Its massive clawed hand grabbed the goat and it slowly backed away. Quietly, calmly, Bea said, "Okay. Slowly get up and back away. Do not make direct eye contact. Do not turn your back to it." I moved like molasses. The beast subtly stiffened as I rose.

I lowered my eyes and instinctively made myself look small. The monstrosity went back to eating the goat. Bea said softly as she pulled me behind her, positioning herself between the creature and me, "That won't last long. We need to get back to camp." As the ape-thing tore into the goat carcass, we made our escape. Bea said that there was no reason to scold me for leaving camp as I had enough punishment in almost being eaten already. She had dropped another goat further back along the trail before dealing with the yeti, so we had food. We decided that moving away from the creature's lair would be best before settling down to cook and eat. We packed up camp and continued our trek into the Tibetan Himalayas. Soon we would find the lost temple.

It was later, coming down the mountain after recovering the *Fabled Ossuary of the Golden Emperor*, that she rescued me again. This time from a band of local communist militiamen. Bea's nerves of steel, indomitable charm, and legendary tolerance for alcohol secured our liberation with a game of Russian roulette with the militia captain. It would be easy to imagine that it was it was a death wish that drove this amazing woman to such heights of grandiose adventure, but one could not be further from the truth. Indeed it was her love of life that was at the heart of who she was. A yearning at the core of her being to sample all that this world had to offer.

End

Chapter Two:

Don Knotts, Nosferatu Hunter: His Secret War.

Don Knotts predicted the assassination of JFK while in a violent mescaline trip outside of a Navajo reservation in New Mexico. It wasn't until morning that we realized it was 1987. That event would mark our last week together. We had been thrown together by the whims of the fates, but it was our unlikely alliance that brought about one of the greatest adventures I had ever been involved in.

Knotts was a troubled man with a stain on his soul that will only be expunged in the blood of nosferatu. There was a demon riding that man and he couldn't break free of it until he killed the master vampire that murdered his one true love: Andy Griffith.

I know what you're thinking: *isn't Andy Griffith still alive*? Clone. Alien clone. There have been seven Andy Griffiths that have all met gruesome ends. The original Andy died in 1968.

That is where our story begins.

Knotts always had a bit of a wild streak. Andy had a way of reigning him in and redirecting that pent up self-destructive energy towards better pursuits. Knotts kept Andy from collapsing in on himself. He drew out the best in Andy. Yes, two men can love one another, bound together in a bond deeper than brotherhood, deeper than war. Like two halves of the same soul in different bodies. They weren't lovers, nothing so tawdry and sensational, what they had was beyond mere sexuality. Both men had a string of women, none of whom could hold the heart of either man for very long. In the end, no one understood either man better than they understood each other.

Andy's death hit Knotts hard. Like a hole through the middle of him. Nothing filled it. There's not enough booze, women, or violence to stop the aching. The world turned to ash for him. The best of who he was died with Andy.

What is Enkidu without Gilgamesh? Who are we when the things that were beautiful in this world are destroyed? We might be broken, we might be villains, or we might just find that we are the heroes we needed all along.

Three days after Andy died, a knock came to the disheveled Knotts' trailer door late into the night. He was awake smoking hash and plowing two *"citizens of Mayberry,"* as the groupies of the television show were called back then. He didn't know their names, nor did he care. It was a distraction, albeit a weak one, from the pain he felt tearing him apart inside. The knock came again, and Knotts twirled and sat up in bed. Grabbing the loaded 38 special that he kept under his bed for emergencies, he yelled at the door, "Hold your horses, now! I'll be there in a minute!" He gestured to the one conscious girl to remain where she was. The other was nude and passed out on the floor in a pile of discarded clothing. He stepped over the sleeping girl and made his way to the door. His eyes narrowed, he cocked the hammer of his revolver and hid it behind his back. He cautiously opened the door and he shouted, "I've already paid Carlos for the hash! It was weak shit anyway, so don't go getting stupid or anything when I open this door!"

He got as far as "Carlos" and his voice caught in his throat. Outside in the shadows an eerie figure lurked. No crickets chirped, no moths fluttered, no frogs croaked, not a single dog barking or cat howling. The night was deathly silent. It was the smell that brought Knotts back to his senses. Like fresh, dark, wet earth. And like something rotting. Old decay. The figure lurched forward.

"Well, ain't ya gonna let me in, Don?" said a voice that was like cold knives into Knotts' heart. "I've had just a *heck* of a day, and I surely could use a place to lay my head." It was Andy but without the earnest and innocent charm, as if something had ripped it out of him and replaced it with something subtle, vicious, and clever.

Knotts blinked and it was on the threshold. Face to face with it. Its eyes had no light behind them, just a wicked hunger. But, how could this not be his best friend? Maybe there was some sort of mistake? Knotts eased the hammer down on his revolver and opened the door wider. He barely managed to mutter, "A-Andy? *How...*"

"Don, *please*! I'm in an awful bad way here! I just need help, Don. *Let me in*." Before he knew it, Don unlatched the door and invited it in. In an instant, it threw the door open and knocked the revolver out of Knotts' hand. The thing's face was a bestial, savage mockery of Andy. It growled through a grisly, fanged, grin. "Well, god damn it, Don. I was beginin' to think you stopped caring."

Just as it was about to set upon him, one of the girls walked in wearing only a bed sheet, "Don, I can't find my panties. Is everything..." The thing whipped around and was on top of her in an instant. Knotts was thrown back violently, smashing a glass end table. He had hurt his head and was finding it difficult to focus. When he recovered, he saw the girl hanging limply by the neck from the distorted, monstrous, gaping jaws of the thing. Blood was everywhere and its metallic smell caught in the back of Knotts' mouth. It was greedily drinking her blood with a wild gluttonous abandon derived as much from the defilement of life as it was from the satiation of animalistic hunger. The thing's eyes had rolled back into its head like a shark's as if it was in the grip of a savage and pure ecstatic state. She was shaking involuntarily as she was agonizingly exsanguinated. Knotts was paralyzed in terror. He couldn't believe this was happening.

The sickening thud she made as it released her from its grip, and she hit the floor dead, pulled Knotts back into nightmarish lucidity. The thing that used to be Andy stood over her, its jaw slowly snapping back into its normal position. The sheet she had been wrapped in was soaked in blood and clung to her mercifully granting her some modesty. Knotts frantically looked around for his gun. As the vampire picked bloody gristle from its fangs, it said, "That's the thing about Chinese, Don. A little bit later and you're hungry again." A scream came from the doorway to the bedroom. It flew into the bedroom and Knotts heard a sickening snap followed by the disturbingly unforgettable sounds of It drinking the life out of a victim.

Knotts leaped at his gun laying on the floor next to the dead Asian girl. He readied it just in time for the thing to step out of the bedroom. "Of course, I love Mexican, Don, but it does give me heartburn." It had a dark red fist-sized knot of something bloody in its hand. That chunk of meat was the girl's heart. It wore a bloody and macabre copy of Andy's grin as it stepped into the room. Up until it saw the gun in Knotts' hand. "Now, what are you going to do with that, Don?"

Knotts couldn't even hear the shots over the sound of his heart pounding in his ears and the scream he let out. In what seemed like the blink of an eye the revolver was empty, the hammer kept making the snap-snap-snap sound as Knotts kept trying to fire an empty gun. The thing was now laying in his bedroom doorway. Knotts shakily rose and stepped cautiously towards its body. He had struck it in the head and blew a chuck of its skull off. But, what was even more impossible to believe than that he had just killed the reanimated corpse of his best friend, was that the wounds seemed to be slowly closing right before his eyes.

Knotts acted quickly. He snatched up a Ronson lighter next to the overturned coffee table and grabbed a recently opened bottle of Bombay gin from the kitchenette counter. When he got back to the body, it was beginning to stiffly convulse and the skull was almost sealed up. He poured every last drop of that gin over the vampiric doppelganger of his friend. As it's bloodshot and murderous eyes shot open, Knotts ignited the lighter and dropped it on what was left of Andy Griffith. The blast was much larger than he had expected. It singed his boxers, undershirt, and the kimono robe Andy had given him in Okinawa. He flew backwards and everything went gray.

The next lucid moment he had was of being outside the trailer, still smoldering from the blast, watching his home burn down with those two girls and whatever was left of that thing. The trailer wasn't in his name. He had been laying low here, in southern California, after Andy's death in Mexico at the hand of crooked federales. Knotts recalled perfectly that cold desert night at that border town truck stop. Andy had sacrificed himself to save Knotts. How could he not remember? It was what he was trying to drown out of his head these past two days with blow, booze, women, and fist fights. But, if Andy didn't die there? If Andy was made into this monster? Why? And by whom? And why did Andy come here? To him?

That's the story as Knotts told it piecemeal over the year or so we traveled together. Bits of detail that would stick in his mind's eye.

There were times when he would sit alone and stare off in the distance with this grim look on his face, and you'd know. He's reliving some tiny facet of that night. The glimmer of the bottle of Bombay gin as it reflected the moon light from outside. The brilliant spark of the lighter before it ignited. The smell of the thing. The sound it made as it fed and the shuddering whimpering sounds the girls made as they died. Piece by piece he would tell me this story as each moment came back to haunt him. As each strobe-lit millisecond froze in impenetrable diamond. It was a living hell. Which is why I believe he did what he did.

I recall exactly when and where Knotts and I first met. Knotts was the sort of man with whom you'd remember the day that special kind of anarchy entered your life. It was November of 1986 in Houston, Texas. I was investigating paranormal activities and hauntings and my research had taken me to a rather rough part of the city. As I was leaving a small corner store, two men approached. I had noticed and began walking faster to cross the street at the corner. Two more men headed me off and blocked my progress. I was surrounded by some very serious looking individuals whom I felt wanted more than some spare change.

That's when fate intervened. From behind the guys on my tail I heard someone say, "Mira, pendejo, leave the kid alone. Because if you've got a problem with him, then you've got a problem with me." I turned to see Knotts standing there. He had a bottle of Jack Daniels in his hand, a five o'clock shadow, a match stick between his teeth, and a mean glint in his eye.

"What's it to you, old man! Get the fuck out of here and go watch *The Price is Right*, or some shit. You are about the get hurt." Said one of the young men. The others laughed and sneered in approval at the derision and dismissed Knotts.

That mean look in his eye turned into a crazed grim grin. Knotts swung that bottle at the nearest banger's head and damn near split the guy's skull open. In a flash, Knotts' other hand produced a butterfly knife that whirled into lethal readiness. I remember its silver gleam in the sunlight. That knife went hilt-deep into the next guy's chest. Where it remained as Knotts then grabbed the pistol the thug had tucked into his waistband. This attack came on so suddenly and so brutally that the gang was stunned for that first bloody moment. But, once two men were down the other two snapped into action and drew their own firearms. I dropped to the ground and scurried for my life between the two gunmen. Seeing as they had larger concerns at the moment, I slipped through just fine.

As the two bangers drew on Knotts, he used the thug with the chest wound as a human shield. Knotts fired from behind him. The bangers plugged their own man as Knotts took them out. What I remember about that is a lot of gunfire, seeing as I was keeping my head down behind a parked pick-up truck at the time. I heard someone walk over to where I was hiding. Imagine my relief when I saw Knotts standing there wiping his knife clean with a handkerchief. "Well, the cops will get here soon. We should probably get the hell out of here."

"Uh, *we*?" was all I could manage.

"Those men I just seriously fucked up beyond all recognition? They were sent here to kill you. You've been asking questions. Someone noticed. But, I need you alive. For now. So, how about we skedaddle while the getting's good?" we headed to his pitch black 1973 Pontiac Firebird Trans Am. The engine thundered as we peeled out and made our way to a safe place.

Knotts told me that he was in Houston on personal business. At this point my research and his business were intersected. When I asked what personal business he was dealing with, he smiled and kept quiet. As we pulled into what was possibly the seediest freeway motel in Houston he said, "Personal means just that. But, seeing as you are walking around with a great big '*come fucking blow my head off*' sign taped to your back, I'll clue you in. Kid, I hunt vampires."

I just sat there wondering if I had heard him correctly. I've seen a lot of weird things. Vampires are not outside the realm of possibility. I mean, I was once almost eaten by a yeti. "Why would gang bangers want to murder me? What does that have to do with vampires?"

"That's the 64 dollar question. We are about to get an answer." He parked the car. We got out and he led me to a corner room on the second floor. Crying children, couples arguing, and loud music poured out of this dump. But it all felt weirdly unreal. As if it was some kind of camouflage for something truly unsettling.

Knotts explained our presence here, "There are only four true oracles in the world. Folks with some kind of direct connections to the powers that be. Every one of them requires an altered state to do what they do and eventually it kills them. Oh, it's not the drugs. A normal human mind can't easily handle messages coming in like freight trains from a place just outside space-time. Tends to fry the circuits and blow out the fuses. This one is different. She's not a normal human.

"I am telling you this so that you don't lose your shit when you see her. You're not going to lose your shit are you, kid?"

"I don't think so." I answered.

"Good. Because she's not from around here and she's got good reason to not like 'mundanes.' Keep quiet, stay behind me, and whatever you do, do not look her in the eyes."

Reflexively, I asked, "Why?"

"Because you'll see your death." We stopped in front of room 217.

He knocked on the door. I heard shuffling inside. He knocked again. The door cracked open without anyone behind it. We entered and Knotts closed the door behind us. The room was dark. Blankets had been pinned up to cover windows. A soft, dim, rosy light filled the motel room. There was a strange sickly sweet smell that hung in the air mixed with cheap sandalwood incense.

Then I saw her. I suddenly became aware of her when she moved, but she had been there the whole time. My mind was having a hard time wrapping itself around that. It was as if she just walked out of a nothingness that never existed to a place she was already standing in. Knotts would later tell me that being around her had a detrimental effect on sanity. The effects were supposedly temporary, but repeated exposure isn't good long term.

"What have you brought here, Don?" Her voice was like being pulled into sleep after a long weary day. It was a voice that could be heard with the ears but also inside your head. It was heartbreakingly beautiful and terrifyingly invasive all at once. As welcome and familiar as the aromas in your grandmother's kitchen and as horrific and alien as a wasp hatching from inside your ear.

"You're the oracle, lady. You tell me." He pulled out a thick envelope from his coat and tossed it on the unmade bed. When she reached for it that's when I saw her. Slender, graceful, fragile. Something was wrong. Something was wrong. She's not *right*. She's not human, right? Oh, God. Oh, God! *Her face*! Alien and ancient. Lips, nose, ears... and *eyes*. So strange. Something was wrong.

Knotts spun around and snapped his fingers loudly in front of my face. "Hey! Kid! Now what did I just get done telling you?" I focused on Knotts' face. He looked annoyed. "Just look down, okay. Look at your shoes." Half still in a daze, I complied. He handed me a piece of gum. "Here, this helps. I don't know why." I took the gum and as I unwrapped it Knotts turned back to the oracle.

She took the envelope without opening it or counting what was inside. "I know it is the usual amount." She said matter-of-factly. As she spoke I focused on chewing gum. It really did help. "They knew you were coming. They heard about this boy asking questions. Strange questions. People talked. The same people who told you about the boy. But, now they know you are close. They think he matters to you. They will try to take him and use him against you."

"Well don't that beat all? I was only interested in the kid because they were." Admitted Knotts. "I am half tempted to just let them have the kid."

"The boy *must* live." The oracle said sternly and with a concrete certitude that was preternatural.

"Why is that now?" Said Knotts, his curiosity piqued.

"I will not say more. Not with him here. He has already begun his quest, though he does not realize it yet." Then, suddenly, I could feel the air just stiffen with an odd chill. There was a feeling like a hand clutching at your heart suddenly squeezing. The oracle's eyes went wide. "They are close! Leave! Now!"

Knotts flew for the door with me in tow. I was still in a confused state and could offer little resistance. When her eyes went wide. Those large almond shaped eyes. Those eyes of inky blackness. They seem to stand out against the alabaster of her skin. In those eyes I saw something. Something coming fast.

***

Let me take a moment here to reflect upon Knotts' musical tastes. He had exactly thirteen cassette tapes in his vehicle. In no specific order: *Transformer* by Lou Reed, *Aftermath* by The Rolling Stones, *Raw Power* by The Stooges, *The Planets* by Gustav Holst, *Raising Hell* by Run-DMC, *Diver Down* by Van Halen, *Back in Black* by AC DC, *Carpenters* by The Carpenters, *Never Mind the Bollocks, Here's the Sex Pistols* by The Sex Pistols, *Songs in the Key of Life* by Stevie Wonder, and a personal mix tape with side A being tracks from Journey's *Escape* and *Frontiers* albums. Side B was mostly Boston (from *Boston*, *Don't Look Back*, and *Third Stage*) with two songs by Kansas (from Point of *Know Return* and *Leftoverture*. You know the ones; the only ones anybody knows.) *Songs in the Key of Life* was a double set, *Carpenters* for the Burt Bacharach medley, and Holst for *Mars, Bringer of War*. Occasionally, he'd listen to the radio, but he hated commercials and absolutely loathed morning radio deejays.

The thirteenth cassette was *Man in Black* by Johnny Cash. Knotts never listened to this cassette; at least, not in my presence. He would pick it up now and then, when looking for music to listen to, and set it back in the shoe box that he used to store his tapes inside of. When I asked him why, all he would say that all he had to do was look at it and every note rang through him as if he were hearing it out loud. For some reason, that he had failed to ever share with me, this cassette was special to him.

***

When we were back in the car, a large white van pulled into the parking lot of the motel. Its windows were tinted and it had no distinguishing markings. I found its very nondescript nature to be somehow perturbing. The car rumbled when the ignition turned and Knotts peeled out in reverse. He didn't even take the time to shift into forward gear, he turned to look out the rear window and drove backwards. "I learned this from a stunt driver who worked on *Bullitt*." He backed out into the street narrowly avoiding oncoming traffic, shifted into forward gear, and then burned rubber down the freeway.

I looked back to see the van bounding out of the motel parking lot and swerving before correcting course to give chase. A light blue, early eighties, Honda Accord slid into the rail and ground brutally to a halt after the van ran it off the road in pursuit of us. We had a good lead, but I still had this lingering sense of dread over the van. The windows were almost completely blacked out; I couldn't make out the driver.

Knotts then gripped the gearshift, "Hang on." he said as he pumped the brake and clutch hard. With a forceful and sharp turn of the steering wheel, Knotts spun the car one hundred and eighty degrees, pointing towards the oncoming van. As the turn was completing he shifted hard again and hit the gas. We were speeding towards the big white van. "In the glove box. Give me the revolver. *Quickly*!"

My heart was racing. I reached forward and opened the glove box. There it was, Knotts' 38 special. "*Now* would be great, kid!" His hand was out waiting for the gun. I took it from the glove box and handed it to him. "Thanks!" He rolled down the driver's side window and shifted the gun into his left hand. "Keep your head down."

The van seemed to move with impossible speed towards us. It seemed unreal and from some strange place inside me an odd laughter seemed to come up unconsciously. I heard the revolver being fired over the roar of the engine and the scream of the wind and road rushing in from the open window. Loud, quick, pops over howling engine and the droning winds. The van swerved to avoid us and Knotts blasted at it as it went by.

One of the van's front the tires exploded leaving a serpentine-like rubber skin and black skid marks on the road. The van shuddered and swerved before flipping completely over, tumbling again and again. The vehicles rear doors flew open and were sheared off in the crash as its glass windows exploded like shimmering rain all over the freeway. Knotts then quickly turned the car around and drove up to the wrecked van that was starting to smolder. We stopped about ten yards away from it. Even from that distance, I could smell engine fluids and gasoline as we pulled up. There was someone trying to open the passenger door of the van from the inside. Knotts withdrew from his ash tray a small box of strike-anywhere matches and got out of the car leaving the driver's side door wide open. He struck one of those matches and tossed it in the path of the tiny river of escaping fuel that was coming from the van. He then turned, quickly made his way back into the car, and we sped off. I looked back and saw that as the passenger door was finally being forced open from within, the entire van was swallowed by an exploding bloom of flame. The force of the blast made it seem to hop slightly, weightless for an instant, like tissue paper cast into a blazing kiln.

Knotts turned to me and let out a heavy sigh of relief. "Whew! What do you want to eat for lunch? I could go for some Mexican." He reached over and placed his revolver back in the glove box. He then selected a cassette from his box and slipped it into the car's cassette player. I saw fire trucks and an ambulance with sirens blaring coming down the other side of the freeway as *Back in Black* started to play.

I was in a little bit of shock and felt my whole body begin to shake uncontrollably. I am not sure if it was the lingering effects of being in the presence of the oracle or post-traumatic shock from the recent round of freeway joust, but all I could muster up was, "Sure. Mexican sounds good."

That was how I met Knotts. As it turned out he was tracking an ancient vampire with possible connections to the very powerful Mexican organized crime ring that was responsible for Andy's death. In Houston, only one such vampire fit the bill: Xochi Quate, also known on the streets as *La Flor Venenosa*. She had taken over several small street gangs under her banner of Hispanic racial superiority. She had ties to the Culebra cartel that controlled illegal activities along the Mexico-Texas border. *La Raza Nueva* was what she called her followers. They were fanatically devoted to her. Each one had earned a tattoo of a feathered serpent over their heart by delivering a family member as a blood sacrifice to her. This was to demonstrate that they belonged to her family now and that all old allegiances, even to blood, were now over. Knotts had hunted vampires all along the border from

California, through Arizona and New Mexico, and the trail had lead him to Texas.

Xochi Quate was stunningly, painfully, beautiful. Her silky raven hair flowed down to her waist. Her olive-complected skin was without blemish of flaw. Her eyes were incandescent pools of crystalline jade that reflected your desire for her, but from which no true love could escape. She had a large, beautifully drawn, elaborate tattoo of a feathered serpent on her back. Her cruelty to those she deemed as unworthy, or beneath her, was legendary; as was her reputation for lavishly rewarding exceptional loyalty and success. She always dressed in the most modern and stylish apparel. She had the cold, dead eyes of a shark and the mind of a Machiavellian chess master. Her anger burned cold like a midnight sun. She was named after an Aztec goddess and carried herself as such. And like an Aztec god, she demanded blood.

But that is a story for another time.

***

One day, nearly a year after our meeting in Houston, Knotts and I were eating lunch at a Waffle House. We were just outside of Tucson, Arizona. I was there to catch a Greyhound bus home. We were quiet for a long while and then, out of the blue, he looks up from his waffle said to me, "Kid, I want to ask you a question. What gives with that spooky laugh you do when shit looks like it's going to hit the fan?"

I thought about it for a moment and said, "Honestly, I have no idea." I hardly looked up from my meal. "I've always just done it. I guess it's as if I *literally* can't believe what's going on around me at those moments. It all seems so profoundly absurd." I poured syrup onto the waffle I had just slathered peanut butter on.

"It used to creep me the hell out." He said as he took a drink of his coffee.

I stopped eating and looked at him. "You hunt vampires and my *tiny*, albeit weird, tick creeps you out?"

"Used to, yeah." He mixed his runny eggs into a bowl of grits and added a dash of tabasco.

"*So...* doesn't anymore?" I inquired.

"Nah. *Now* what creeps me out is that you put peanut butter on your waffles. Gross." He took a huge bite of his concoction and smiled as he chewed.

"Whatever, dick, you eat grits." I retorted, as I added more syrup and took another bite.

With a nearly full mouth he sputter-mumbled, "Grits are good. Little butter, mix in some gravy. Good."

"Well, it looks like snot." I washed down my lunchtime breakfast with a tall glass of ice-cold whole milk.

"*S'not* bad at all." He said with a clever, not-so-sheepish, and subtly coy smile. A rare thing. This was our last meal together. In spite of all the grit and blood during our time together, wearing that mischievous and affable smile is how I will always envision Knotts in my mind's eye.

End

Chapter Three:

"Good beginnings are the resting place for the unfinished dreams."

> ~ RH Carroll

"Ibis headed Thoth gave us writing and doomed man to forgetfulness."

> ~ RH Carroll

This chapter might require some explanation. I get lots of ideas throughout an average day. Some of them survive long enough to become really interesting seeds for stories. Most of those story seeds, however, never get any further. Here, I've placed some of those beginnings; as well as a bit of poetry, essays, letters never sent, and projects for games.

I think there is still some beauty in the fragments presented. Should I never get another chance to write, never have to opportunity to expand upon them, they deserve some exposure. However, it might be better to withhold some of these ideas and take some time to present polished pieces.

In any case, I hope you find them to be enjoyable, fun-sized reads.

Time & Space: The Mechanics of Time and Dimensional Travel

We imagine time as a river, moving from the past towards the future, sweeping us along in the present. The current of this mighty river seems immutable and persistently moving with indomitable force in one direction. From the cradle to the grave we are its prisoner being moved along like a leaf caught in its current. We live with the knowledge that there is no going back, no second chances.

We often wonder, "What if?" What if we had turned right instead of left, or called that girl instead of going out with friends, or bought the roast beef instead of the chicken. We will never know and can only presume and dream the possibilities.

But what if it weren't so? What if the fabric of the universe and the mutability of time were much more plastic that we imagined? The natures of trans-dimensional and time travel are inextricably linked. Each and every choice we make spawns a host of new universes and divergent time streams. Each optional universe overlapping and existing alongside our own, moving right next to us, but obscured by the rules of our universe. This effect is called The Veil. It is the imperceptible wall that hides universes from one another. Under ordinary circumstances no one could see it or through it. Under ordinary circumstances no one can move beyond it, as one could step from one room into the next. If everything in our universe is working correctly, we never even know it exists.

I have this vision. I see all the galaxies as blossoms of gravity and mass radiating out along branches of dark matter that spread out like cracks in a pane of glass from the hyper-dimensional trans-temporal "point" in time-space from which it all began. Each star a node connected to all other points.

Oubliette (Formerly Untitled Poem, Number One)

ah, but what price parlaying with oblivion?
it cost a piece of me.
the brilliant part of my childhood,
the glimmer of innocence,
the magic and wonder of a new world.

floating motes of dust drifted like a sea of stars
in the shafts of light that came through the blinds.
the swaying trees outside the window danced for me.
the spider webs in the window pane glistened
like silver threads in a dream.

all that is gone
except for the half remembered dream.

a child bravely sails into darkness.
was it naiveté or arrogance?
courage born of necessity?

what did i gain from my time
in the place of forgetfulness?
a shred of wisdom,
the key to secrets,
a tattered and worn map
to guide me through the labyrinth
of you.

my eyes were changed.
darker though they see more.
blinded to wonder,
now i see secrets
kept in the dark places.

my secret is what i keep
locked away in the deepest vaults
of my heart.
that im lost
and seeking
my way back
to being that child
again.

Untitled Poem, Number Two

look upwards,
turn to face the divine.
i have been contemplating the infinite and the infinitesimal.
the total sum of all things moving in cycles so grand
as to be lost in our meager view.
we, as part of the infinite,
become infinite.
we extend along the upward and inward
axis beyond conceptualization,

beyond language to describe,
beyond mere dimension.

lost like a dream.
a dark spot in vision
created by the momentary spark
now gone.

I Am

*"Kalo 'smi loka-kshaya-krit pravriddho lokan samahartum iha
pravrittah."*

> ~ Quote from the Bhagavad Gita

"I am a hired assassin. It is the only thing I've ever been good at. I
killed my first human being at the age of ten. A man who had been
abusing my mother. I found a large kitchen knife and rammed it
through his back until it came out his front. The only thing I really
remember is the smell of his blood, rich and dark, flowing out of him.
A coppery smell in the back of my throat.

"I wasn't a cruel child. I never hurt small animals. I never set fires. I
obeyed my mother. I was quiet. I spent most of my time looking out
the window at the other children play. I remember that I would often
draw pictures of mythological creatures. I learned to read early and
enjoyed Aesop's fables and books about heroes and monsters. Even
though I was a very still and calm little boy, there was still a deep
reservoir of rage inside me. All in all, childhood was lonely.

"My mother never looked at me the same way again after I ran the
man through. She didn't abandon me per se, but she was a walking
ghost in my life. I left home when I was seventeen. I didn't have
anywhere to go, but there was nothing to stay for. No one came
looking for me.

"I have had many teachers. Many masters. I learned to channel my
will through my body and make it into a weapon. I move with lethality
and grace. I become death. I excelled at ending life. It really is quite

beautiful. This is not braggadocio. Maybe it's a warning. Maybe it is the rattle before the strike.

"I've never known the love of a woman, even though I've been with plenty. A brief and mutually agreed upon arrangement. Clean and efficient. I suppose the women I lay are as professional as I am. In and out, no questions, no clues, no regrets. All of them blur together in my memory like the scent of jasmine on the night air.

"I don't drink. I don't smoke. I don't have friends. I have associates. I have acquaintances. I have clients. I have people to kill. I have no illusions as to the nature of what I do. I do not imagine that anyone I kill is deserving of it. It's not my concern. I do what I agree to do, and then I get paid.

"When I take a life I do not feel anything. No fear, no anger, no guilt, no regret, no pleasure, no arousal. I'm not numb, I am simply there. 'Mushin no shin' as one sensei put it.

"This is the final reverie of the dying. The moments of my life slipping by like droplets of water down a single spider's strand. These will be the last thoughts going through my mind as I lay here. On the cold ground. In the rain. Even now I do not feel anything. Not even the pain of the belly wound as I bleed out. There is, however, a strong coppery smell in the back of my throat."

Honesty

I don't need you to fix me. I don't want you to change who I am, because you'd rather I were different. The only person who can repair the holes in me is me. I like me; and that took a long, hard time to finally learn. But, I want to be a part of what makes you happy. I want to touch you in simple ways. Like the reflex when someone you trust takes your hand and you squeeze back. I want respect, and kindness, and comfort. I want someone who can appreciate just how pervy I am. How silly I am. How hard I try. How much like a child I can be.

The trick is to not trick yourself out of happiness. We deserve happiness. Love forgives. Especially silly fears from an injured heart. I love you. I've forgiven you. Sometimes it takes a while, but it does.

You love yourself, you'll forgive yourself for the imagined crime of not being good enough by your parents misinformed standards. And you'll forgive them for being shitty parents because they honestly didn't know better and were already broken inside long before you were born. Because you'll realize love is better than regret.

***

I found myself eating breakfast at a fast food restaurant today. This one was, like most others, coated in a thin sticky residue of human resignation. Eyes, blankly looking forward. In line. Behind the register. Over the French fry machine. No one comes here deliberately.

It was here I attempted to recall the last time I felt a stirring of wonder in my heart. I remembered the Watchman movie trailer with the Smashing Pumpkins soundtrack. Seeing the comic book come to life with its menagerie of the incredible.

My mind leapt back to a time when I was a small child. A dark summer night on the beach. The luminescent waves advancing and receding. Looking upward I saw the night sky afire. My heart veritably shook and my eyes reeled. I forgot to breathe, and overcome by awe I ran back to the beach house.

My reverie ended as I gazed into the layers of my breakfast sandwich, bite missing, in my hands. This then came to me:

"Make our wonders real and we will worship you. Give voice and form to our most treasured dreams. For, what else is a god for?"

***

I could say that I was always afraid that you would leave me, but that's not true. I was afraid that you would leave us: any family we might build. It's why we never had children. It's why I was hesitant to give you all of me again after you hurt me so badly.

While I might forgive your cruelty towards myself, I just couldn't bear the thought that you'd direct your dark and broken heart at its worst to any child of mine. But the only part anyone will ever know is the lie where you blame me for everything, and the only part I feel is the horrible loss of it all.

***

Don't talk. Just listen. I love you. I forgive you. I forgive us. You're going away. It's okay. The memories of what we were live on forever inside us. Guiding us along our paths. Maybe, if fortune blesses us, those memories will nudge us, ever so gently, back together every now and again. And, with every parting, a new star to guide us. To remind us that we are capable of true love; to remind us that that capability is the greatest part of being human.

***

The things we lose weren't meant to be ours in the first place and there's no peace of mind to be had until you find the good grace to let them go.

I've got no time for someone who avoids conflict. Someone who hides instead of speaking honestly and directly. Someone who refuses show or earn respect. I value discourse and an opportunity to see another point of view, but that will never happen without confrontation.

I forget sometimes that I know who I am, what I've survived, and that I possess unique gifts. Amongst those gifts: great courage in being honestly who I am and refusing to be anything less, ferocious tenacity and a drive to survive even when it would be simpler and less painful to lay down, and a keen mind that perceives things that the vast majority of humanity can't or won't see.

It can be easy to forget. The pain I endure on a near constant basis would destroy most people. The horrors I've witnessed can be impossible to forgive. The seared scars of those days do not fade quickly. The loneliness can become a self-imposed imprisonment. The fear of how savage humans can be, myself included, can be wrought into bars with little effort. It's so very easy to keep silent; to cling to a false safety with a gag in our mouths. The weight of our unhappiness can make risk seem unjustifiable. Slavish pragmatism born of a multitude of simple fears can stifle us and make us resentful too quickly.

There are precious few who know, love, understand, appreciate, accept, and sometimes even forgive me for who I am. All humans long for connection. If you find my introspection tedious, feel free to unfriend me. I understand; there's nothing to forgive.

The things we lose were never meant to be ours in the first place.

November

Another birthday approaches. And I, in this time of great personal change, reflect on the loves of my life. That even what were, at the time, the most painful moments, will transform with the accrual of years into kinder bittersweet memories. For it was wonderful to have been so young, to trust so easily, to be able to have given and received love with such openness. Wonderful to have possessed such potential. And I feel grateful for the wisdom gained, hard earned, that I now possess. I wonder at what the future will reveal to me, for there is much potential left.

Love, or the things we mistake for love, these things are never really in vain. Win or lose, we learn with each new spring and every winter, more of who we really are.

Psychedelic Rockabilly Steampunk Sky Pirates

"Do not dally at the confectionery, Sally! You've got three whole cents, and you'll not spend them all on sweets!" Her mother chastised her with the shrill voice that only mothers can make. The voice that freezes the soul and sears the spine. But, young Sally MacArthur did not crave candied gum drops this day, oh no. Nor did she seek ribbons for dolls' hair, like most boys wrongly supposed. This fine morning was the day that *Doctor Monstositus's Parlour of Terror* came to the shelves of *Old Man Phipp's General Store*. Within these slightly yellowed pages all manner of nightmarish ghoul and ghastly spectre prowled. *Adventure! Wonder! Thrills!* The brightly colored cover promised. It beckoned with a nearly electric shimmer. *Only three red cents*.

I Wrote a Joke

A penguin, a senator, and a toaster walk into a doctor's office. The penguin attempts to initiate a conversation with the toaster. The toaster just sits there. The penguin talks louder assuming the toaster didn't hear him. The toaster just sits there. The penguin starts to get insulted and demands the toaster acknowledge him. The toaster just sits there.

Exasperated, the penguin turns to the senator and asks, "Can you believe the nerve? I think that toaster must be racist. In this day and age! What do you think, senator?"

The senator responded, "I think I need to stop dropping acid at Ihop."

I Love Roleplaying Games!

"B----'s *Bodacious* Brofist, not to be confused with R---'s Radical Respek-Knuckles, which had more in common with Hallister's Hallucinatory High-Five, was a spell designed to reward courage and encourage camaraderie on the battlefield by war wizard captains. Unlike the other two, Hallister's Hallucinatory High Five had more practical applications."

Dollmyr, Caranor Theobrum. "Better Battlefield Cantrips." *Advanced Theurgical Tactics and Revue* 21.11 (2785 CE): 557-618. Print.

Hallister's Hallucinatory High Five is a 0-level spell which has the somatic components of a wink and a smile as you shoot your index finger and thumb at the intended target like a gun, and the verbal component of speaking aloud "*All you, buddy. Up top!*" It yields a temporary +1 bonus to one save, attribute, or skill roll that relies on confidence or camaraderie for a single roll. It may be banked until needed for the duration of the spell. Its duration is one round per caster level. While multiple castings from the same caster (until 8 hours of rest have passed) do not stack bonuses, cast again from another magic-user grants an additional use of the +1 bonus so long as the duration of that spell is not exceeded. Range: 30 feet. No save (beneficial)

Savasana

"Savasana" will be a story about human colonization before FTL, when cryogenic stasis chambers for the long sleep of a millennial journey was the only way.

Seeds cast off of a choking, starving, dying home-world. Set adrift by a desperate prayer of hope. Awakened in an unimaginably savage future, where the only weapon against a tide of evil is a single remaining seed of hope.

A man out of time must become the man of tomorrow.

Will he or she save the world, or rule it? Hurl fuel into the flames of earth's funeral pyre, or forge a new world from the ashes? Will he transform that fire into a light held high to lead the way for all those in the dark?

Amanda, Fourteen Years Gone By

Nothing to forgive. We all have our own labyrinths to find our way out of. I loved you. Because that love was true, it lingers despite the passage of years or the miles between us. So earnestly felt that it needn't be reciprocal to remain integral. In friendship, there is nothing to forgive.

I dropped out. It was made clear that I didn't belong. And for over a decade, I wandered through life. I returned home after a serious respiratory illness. *If I am to die, by God, it will be in Texas*. It's a very Texan way to feel. I feel it and I'm a socialist atheist who shuns the concept of nationalism. Worked retail, sold books, mostly working in comic book shops. Zombie shuffle in the rat race.

Tried hard to resurrect my old life. But that season had passed. Mom died. Had to learn how to walk truly alone in this world. Got engaged. Lasted five years. We're still friends. But it was as if a great storm had picked me up and set me down far from home.

Recently in a position to start over again. This time say yes more. This time I know who I am. I began to write after loosening my last job. I love writing. I love who I am when I write. Passion and wonder returned to my life. I feel alive again for the first time in a very long time.

There is one piece of you that remains in my heart that I included in my book. A character, a captain, she has these eyes. Smokey pools of dark amber honey that are the heart of her wide, honest, beautiful smiles. I love those eyes, especially when they smile. So much so that I made them immortal in a book.

That's as close as I can get to stealing the keys of Solomon and singing a new world into being with the secret language of angels, with which the world was made. Just for you.

I think I am going to be just fine now. Because you are alive, healthy, and I hope very happy. We can be friends I hope.

Goodbyes

On the day my mother died I went to see her at the hospital. The doctors said that there was no way she could have any brain activity. The medications and machines were all that kept her heart beating. I was left in the room alone to say my goodbye. I kissed her forehead and brushed her hair back. She used to do the same for me when I was small and sick.

I could feel that she was trapped inside that body in agony, unable to see out of her blankly staring eyes. It broke my heart to see that. I wish that she could have gone peacefully in her sleep without fear or pain. The woman who had been so vibrant and stubborn just lingering between life and death; unable to escape her bodily prison. Not until the medications wore out and her heart came to a rest.

I spoke to her in her ear, hoping that somewhere inside she could hear and understand. I said that she should not be afraid. That she was not alone. That she was loved. I told her that she was a good person and a good mother. I told her that she had fought longer and harder than anyone could ever ask or expect. That she earned her rest and it was okay to let go. I said to her that she would go and see the face of God. That He would know her as His own daughter. That He would embrace her and take her into Paradise. That she would know no pain and no sorrow ever again. I told her that I would be good. I told her that I would miss her. I stroked her hair and said good bye.

Chapter Four:

I Shall Make a Holocaust of My Heart

A cloudy late-autumn day. Pin prick icy droplets of rain fall sparingly from a withholding sky as red and golden leaves are blown by on the wet ground.

A cemetery. Inside its iron-wrought black gates, a funeral is taking place. Solemn attendees stand silent as the eulogy is given.

Just outside the cemetery, an extreme right wing fundamentalist church protests. Whole families chanting hateful slogans. Children holding up signs with hurtful, ignorant things on them.

A lone car from the sheriff's department sits not too far off to observe and keep the peace. Inside, a single deputy sat, numbed to the disgusting sideshow. He was lost in his newspaper as a small hand radio buzzed about sports. Routinely, a voice would squawk across the police radio installed in the vehicle and he would respond blandly that there was nothing new to report.

A single figure in a dark navy coat, faded blue jeans, and worn work boots approaches the protesters. He makes his way into their midst, past the house wives who scream that he's going to hell in fanatical ecstasy. He goes to the loudest most fervent one. The one screaming into a bull horn.

"*You don't need to be here.*" He spoke quietly and looked directly into the lead protester's eyes with a startling sincerity. His words were lost in the din, but he captured the attention of the self-proclaimed prophet.

"Please leave. What you are doing is wrong. You desperately need to ignore the fact that these are human beings you are tormenting. You require this delusion to prop up the faulty framework of crackpot theology your parents force-fed you. Without that broken and shoddy belief system, what are you? I know you dread the alienation you would face for listening to the tiny voice inside telling you that being here and doing this is wrong. But, if you listen to that little voice and pack everyone up, and leave quietly, you'll know a measure of true happiness. And," he adds ominously, "You'll not have to face the consequences for remaining.

He looks deeply into her eyes, smiles softly, and with great pity for her, asks after a long beat, "Do you know who I am?" She nods slowly turning pale with fright, nearly frozen in terror. "You see, Yeshua was our father's compassion and a chance at redemption. He was His love made manifest. All you have to do is as he asks. Be kind. Love one another. What is the greatest commandment? Love God with all of your being. The second greatest? Love one another as He loves you all. You see, because God is within all of us. So when you spit, and curse, and harass anyone, you're doing that to Him. Even to the very least of His flock. Yes, Yeshua resisted his purpose at Gethsemane. He had a choice. And he chose to honor his purpose: Love. For you.

"Yeah, Yeshua was His love.

"*I am not.*

"I am my father's wrath. I am my father's retribution made manifest. But, I don't want to be. Right now, I'm a terrified, broken, nobody. Alone, poor, in pain. But, I have free will. I have to choose to become what my father made me to be. Like Gethsemane. Once I choose to follow that path, all I will ever be is written in stone. Yeshua was our father's hammer with which a bridge might be built, but I am His terrible flaming sword. I'm pleading with you. *Please.* Don't make me choose today."

End

Chapter Five:

A Conversation with Sam Wicker

"You're probably noticing the horns. It's the horns isn't it? Or my eyes? No, it's okay. I am quite used to it. I used to be self-conscious about these features, but now I see and appreciate them for what they are. First of all, they are a warning. They let people know not to fuck with me. Secondly, and I really love this, they serve as asshole detectors and repellants.

"I mean, I look like a devil. The horns, the eyes, the ears, the tail; they all scare the shit out of idiotic drunken yokels looking to blow off steam or fleece easy marks. They aren't about to go poking what they can only assume is a big demonic hornets' nest. Which, when you think about it, makes them just a sliver smarter than they look.

"And if anyone were to be in a mood to make trouble with me because of my appearance, well, that's a huge indicator that they are someone best kept at arm's length. Even better kept at the exact length of a rope and noose. It filters out the hayseeds, rubes, and clowns. That is genuinely useful in my line of work.

"I work with all sorts. Mercenaries and treasure hunters of all stripes. You might say my predicament grants me a more egalitarian world view. If someone is of use, then they are welcome to stick around. But, *you know*, at an appropriate distance.

"Paladins may have their place in the battlefield; wading through the muck and blood, waving banners, and kneeling before statues of this god or that god. They win wars for well-fed kings and their fat, spoiled nobles... but you'll see precious few on the streets where the poorest live. Precious few making any *real* difference. You can keep paladins.

"I was raised in an orphanage. The kind of orphanage that would take an oddity such as myself in. To their credit, the sisters did their best to keep me fed and clothed, to put a roof over my head. However, the pedantic chatter about my eternal soul wore thin *fast*. Especially when meals were little more than thin gruel and my clothes were little better than rags. The other children and a few of the more, shall we say, *enthusiastic* nuns, made sure to remind me that I was different. They said *worthless*, *evil*, *wicked*, or *tainted*. And some even backed up their positions with the occasional back hand or balled fist. But I knew they meant *better* and that they feared what made me better. The only good thing about that place was the sisters went to bed early and the locks were cheap. I could sneak out and back in before anyone awoke.

"It was on the streets at night that I learned how to survive. How to use my abilities to their fullest. How to find worth in who I was. Maintaining the illusion of a suitably chastised urchin taught me to be meticulous and disciplined. My early years taught me to rise above the brutishness and squalor I was raised in. I acquired a code to live by. Good or evil doesn't matter. Survival matters. Power matters. Knowledge matters. Because they are all the same thing. If you become a threat to my survival, I will eliminate you. Once the other inmates at the orphanage understood that, things got a lot easier.

"Don't misunderstand, I'm not looking for trouble. I am not psychotic. A string of corpses is bad for business. If a friendly talk will get the job done, I am a regular chatterbox. But should it prove necessary to perforate your heart with a stiletto, you'll never see it coming. It doesn't matter who you think you are; kings and paupers all die just the same.

"I was adopted by a wizard in my 13th year. I suppose he saw my potential. He was a hard man of few words, but he was fair. He punished me when I failed to fulfill my responsibilities and rewarded me when I exceeded them. On my 18th year he retired and released me from my apprenticeship. He died last year. Some fat greedy noble claimed my master's wealth as *tax* because he had no *legal* heirs. I suppose being some sort of half-devil makes me ineligible.

"I suppose the greatest gift the old wizard gave me was liberation from that lice-infested shit hole and the knowledge he imparted to me. Still, I just might rob that slothful pig-faced noble of every coin he has... I *might* not even kill him. Just to see his face when he realizes that his treasury is empty.

"Recently, I have begun a quest to unravel the mysteries of my origin. The year before I arrived at the orphanage, there was a scandal in the noble houses. Young noble women of alleged saintly virtue were whisked away to nunneries for periods close to nine months. Several of these so-called noble houses have less than reputable pasts. Perhaps my birth was an unpleasant reminder that the chickens had come home to roost. Regardless, arranged marriages were annulled, duels were fought, wars nearly broke out, hilarity ensued. Now that's what I call an *auspicious* birth.

"Clerics serve a purpose, I suppose. When they aren't trying to proselytize ad nauseam, they do manage to heal injuries, sickness, and other infirmities. At the very least, some of these priests, when not bilking the naïve out of hard earned coin, *do* actually help those who need help in the worst parts of the city. Plus, you've really got to hand it to them; it is a very effective grift. I mean, giving them your hard earned scratch equals entrance to a paradise *after* you die and all that crap. Pure genius. People *want* to believe that drivel.

"Dwarves. Reliable. Not so much fun, but you can count on a dwarf to get a job done. You can also count on a dwarf to hold a grudge. If you're smart, and I am, *very*, all it takes is to nudge that grudge in the right direction and then sit back.

"The law? Useful. *When* it can be made to serve you. Usually, it can. Most city guardsmen know about as much about the law as I know about being a stupid clod whose only employment outlook was to be some oafish city guardsman. I have a code I live by. It may not necessarily be *your* code. It works for me and I stick to it. If wanted to be some poor, sheep-herding, goat-fornicator; well, then I guess I would live by rules someone else made for me. But I don't. Incidentally, get a city guardsman drunk enough and he'll fornicate with just about any four legged barn animal you put into a dress. I have a theory that the ale consumption is merely a pretense that hides a thinly veiled lust for beasts in most of these constabulary types.

"But I digress. The law has nothing to do with anything except making sure that the powerful stay powerful, and the powerless are bled dry. I'd rather have that kind of power on my side; or understand it well enough to turn it back on the corpulent obtuse nobles. It's a wonderful trick getting the impoverished to believe that laws protect them, I am amazed that people as scat-for-brained as the noble castes pulled it off.

"What do *I* enjoy? Oh, I don't know, the same things anyone does. Good food, good drink, good clothes, beautiful women, games of chance... which aren't *really* chance if you can read the other players, play using your head, and maybe rig the game.

"Fighting. Avoid it if possible. A fair fight is a sucker's bet. Use *every* advantage. Bite, claw, kick them in the junk, whatever works. Never go out unarmed, never sit with your back to a door or window, never drink with people you don't trust, never drink from a bottle you didn't handle, never take someone's word that the dice aren't loaded, and *never* pet a donkey on Thursdays. (Okay, that last one I made up just to see if you were listening.) There is no better time to kick a man than when he is down, one well-placed sniper is worth a whole army, know yourself and your enemy, and never *ever* give away anything for free.

"Love. Have I ever loved? Yes. That's all I have to say about that. Most people confuse love with something else: infatuation, affection, lust. Love is a choice. A commitment. It's easy to just chalk love off as something that is made up, but it's not. It's real. That's why people use it against you. When they do, it's a deadly thing. I won't let that happen again.

"What *about* forgiveness? The sisters used to rattle off platitudes about forgiveness being divine and what not, but they did precious little forgiving. I don't really believe in mystical automatic redemption. Just saying you're sorry doesn't hack it. You *must* atone. There are, however, some things cannot be forgiven. My master gave me a book once and it said that forgiveness is an act of mercy, which it isn't done because people deserve it, but rather because they need it. What *I* needed was a family and a home. *I* need not to be chased out of every place I visit because of my features. *I* need my rightful inheritance. I need... well, when I get what I need, I *might* consider giving a little. Until then, the anger keeps me warm.

"*Friendship*? Remember what I said about love? Yeah. I have acquaintances, clients, and associates. I wouldn't call any of them *friends*. A friend is someone who has your back. Always. *Especially* when there is nothing to gain and *everything* to lose. When I find someone like that, I'll let you know.

"Heroes. You think I do this for the glory or because if I don't it makes baby kittens cry? Being heroic is thankless. Graveyards of *full* of heroes. Glory fades. I am in it for the coin. Sometimes, *rarely*, I am in it because some prick rubs me the wrong way. Even rarer still, I am in it because someone did someone else wrong. I wouldn't call it heroic. The last thing you are thinking about when facing imminent mortality is how you'll get *so* much trim from awestruck wenches for what you are doing. You are sometimes *literally* shitting yourself and praying to gods you don't believe in to spare your life from the monstrosity that wants to kill, fuck, and eat you. In that order.

"Someone once said, 'The world is wrong and every day folks learn a little more how to accept it the way it is. It's heartless and brutal. But that's why there are heroes. It doesn't matter where they came from, or what they've endured, or if they even make a difference. They refuse to accept the world the way it is. They fight against the corrupt status quo. They live as though the world were as it should be to show it what it could be... I think I read that on a tombstone."

End

Chapter Six:

Karl

Karl wasn't like the other goblins, here, in the Ruined and Befouled City of Mal-wonk-kee. The locals left off the honorifics and just called it Malwonkee, but to Karl this place and those words were inseparable. Every day he spent here hammered that truth deeper into his mind. Unlike other goblins he had dreams, hopes, and aspirations. Karl dreamed that one day, he might open his own land-based sting ray farm. It was an inexplicable and persistent dream that was as distant as the fabled Crumbling Mountains of the Elder Beasts; for sting rays only lived under water. So Karl sat lost in thought at the diner, at the corner of East Erie and North Water, and he drank what was left of his slowly cooling and increasingly dissatisfying coffee. Karl tossed a few copper coins on the counter near his half-full cup of once-hot coffee. He had lingered in reverie for far too long. With a deep and regretful exhalation, He said to himself: *Come on Karl. It's time to stop dreaming and just live the life you've got*. He heaved himself off of the stool he was perched upon and pushed himself (with a slight limp) out the door.

Winter was fast approaching and the city was, as always, stained in scuzzy yellows and grungy browns. The gray and dirty winter slush on the ground matched the equally dismal skies, locked in a joyless haze for the duration of this season of deathless slumber. One must step cautiously lest they slip on ice or fall into pot holes filled with icy muck-water. The biting cold made every day here a trial of the will to step outside the front door. It was the kind of place that required a mournful sigh, like a brief and ardent orison for mercy before venturing out.

As Karl walked back to work, he was lost in thought. He felt that opening his dream farm on New Mars was too abstract a concept to be taken seriously. Stepping into the river of pedestrians on the sidewalk, Karl waded into the throng of monsters. He moved against the current of foot traffic on the street like a fish struggling to swim upstream. He was only partially aware of the giant flaming rock hurtling towards him from the stars. The ominous object lingered on the periphery of his senses like so many street vendors, rickshaws, and beggars. Indeed, even the cries of terror from nearby pedestrians barely registered whilst Karl day dreamed of an impossible, better tomorrow.

As Karl slowly became aware of his impending doom, he thought to himself in the tiniest sliver of moments: Huh. Well, I certainly never thought it would end like this. No one was more surprised than Karl himself when the hurling mass of star-stuff came to an abrupt halt a mere twelve inches from his awestruck face. Paralyzed in disbelief, Karl stood there, mesmerized by the shimmering, humming monolithic object that floated, oxymoronically, like a butterfly above his perplexed noggin.

Time had ceased to have any real meaning or context for Karl, who in a matter of milliseconds went from melancholic longing to profound stunned acceptance of his own mortality. Eventually, Karl became aware that there was a bellowing voice coming from the sphere. A trumpeting voice that blew back Karl's hair and hummed through his coffee-stained teeth. By the time Karl had regained his wits and could comprehend what the giant ball of fire was roaring, this is what he heard: "... IS YOUR SACRED MISSION! GO FORTH, KARL SNOTWALLER AND FOLLOW YOUR DESTINY!"

Just as Karl began to utter the phrase "Excuse me, would you mind terribly repeating all that?", the giant orb of flaming loudness blinked out of existence leaving behind a mighty gust of wind knocking down signs and rubbish bins, blowing newspapers and posted bills hither and thither, and further disheveling Karl's hair and clothing.

Karl looked around and saw that the previously packed street was now seemingly abandoned. A lonesome tumbleweed meandered across the intersection of East Erie and North Water for what seemed like a silent eternity. Slowly, the denizens of Malwonkee reappeared. Squinched goblinoid faces poked out of doorways and cautiously peeked out of windows. A stick with a hat dangling of its end was shakily thrust from behind an overturned apple cart. In the distance dogs confusedly barked as if to reassure themselves that they still existed. Gradually, goblins, gremlins, trolls, and all manner of folk in this cosmopolitan quasi-pandemonium, this metropolis of the unsavory, this city of minor monsters and b-level horrors returned to the area to resituate themselves post... er... post-flaming-screaming-ball-of-whatever-that-was-anyway.

Karl would soon discover that any witnesses to the event would claim that all that had emanated from the alleged cosmic death ball was a blast of noise and wind. Most onlookers assumed that it had simply obliterated its target and, in a freak occurrence, left everything else mostly unharmed. No one could be absolutely sure; as nearly all who saw the object hurling towards the area were occupied with fleeing for their lives. No one could recall any words being spoken or destinies being forged. The authorities would later claim that it was all simply sewer gas. A resource which Malwonkee possessed in abundance.

***

Karl awoke with a start. As sleep slowly withdrew its grip on him, he became gradually aware that he was in his own dingy little bed. After a few nervous moments, he realized it was all just a dream. A bowel-shakingly intensely realistic and unsettling dream. A heavy sigh of relief left him and he climbed out of bed.

As he was having his deeply satisfying morning movement, reading yesterday's Sunday comic strip, his phone rang. Clearly, this looks like a job for the answering machine, he thought to himself as he continued reading about the adventures of *Streetknight the Masked Paladin.*

The machine picked up. The click and whir of the answering machine's outgoing message began. "This is Karl. Uh, should you need to... uh, wait... if you'd like to leave a message, please –BEEP!"

"I have *got* to make a better outgoing message." he said to himself as he listened to the machine in the next room.

"Karl! Hey, uh, '*buddy*'. You feeling okay?" it was Karl's boss, Psycho Joe, sounding uncharacteristically, and yet with a definite undertone of complete insincerity, concerned. "Yeah, well. I've, uh, I've got bad news, guy." PJ cleared his throat, "As of today we will no longer be requiring your services. (Well, that went rather well, I'd say.) So, um, don't you go and do anything rash okay? It's just that a guy who talks about flaming balls of destiny just isn't a good fit here at *Tombstone Books and Other Pointless Junk Shoppe*. So, you are invited to not return. Ever. Mr. Tombstone sends his regards and wishes you the best of lu- aw, fuck it. –CLICK!"

Karl sat there on his toilet in a bit of a panic. Which was probably a tiny bit of good fortune, because if he had been anywhere else he'd have shit himself. *Hooray for small favors*, he thought sarcastically.

Upon replay Karl could definitely make out the sound of the muffled laughter of his other co-workers. He expected that kind of behavior from Kire the Sanctimonious, but Little Lolo too? Well, after the initial shock wore off and before the 38th replay of the message, Karl actually started to feel a little relieved. After the 116th replay, he felt downright positive about his prospects. After all, wasn't this just supposed to be a part-time job that had become a full-time gauntlet of his co-workers' paranoid neuroses and narcissistic delusions of grandeur? Sure, the money would be missed, but overall, he wouldn't miss very much about Tombstone.

"Yup, the future is now, Karl Snotwaller!" He said to himself reassuringly and with the confidence of a free goblin with nothing left to loose.

Verna T. Roache was Karl's land lady. She was a rare species of giant sentient sapient louse. No sooner had Karl resolved that this change was probably some sort of blessing in disguise did she come knocking at the door. The thing about Mrs. Roache was that she never waited for anyone to actually come to the door before barging on in. The jangle of her ring of keys signaled that she would simply allow herself in. The door opened on Karl just standing next to his answering machine, Sunday funnies still in hand, and one finger on the answering machine playback button, and his boxers around his ankles.

"Heard the news. You've got thirty days to find a new job or you're out. I don't abide free loaders and parasites. And put some pants on! I don't abide *perverts* either!" She slammed the door behind her and stormed upstairs to her apartment on the top floor.

The door rebounded with a reverberating thud off of the door frame and swung wide open as his neighbor across the way, Janice, came home from her morning workout. Karl had always had a small crush on Janice, but never made any kind of move. At first because he was seeing someone, but after she left him for a bridge troll, he just never felt like the time was right. Janice looked shocked, appalled and a little nauseated. She quickly entered her apartment, and loudly turned every single one of the thirty-seven bolted locks on her door into the locked position in rapid succession. Then her emergency panic blast-door came down with a rumbling thud.

Karl pulled up his boxers, closed his front door, and with forehead leaning against the recently shut door said, "This will not end well." He wasn't sure. But he thought he could hear Janice's safety whistle shrilling from inside her apartment.

He spent the remainder of the day in a depressed torpor on his couch, in his boxers, watching reruns of old shows and eating cereal out of the box. That night he washed down some allergy pills with a beer and hoped that tomorrow would be better. He has a month to find work or hit the road.

***

The next day Karl awoke when a knock came to his door. He surmised that it wasn't Old Widow Roache when this person didn't immediately break and enter his domicile. Karl spun his feet off the edge of the bed, sat up and rubbed the grit from his eyes. He glanced at his alarm clock on the bedside table. It was a little after 2 pm. He had slept right through the morning.

There came a second knock at the door and Karl rose up to go see who it was. "I'm coming, just a minute!" He hollered as he threw on his worn and faded red bathrobe, with the holes in the too-small waist pockets, and stumbled his way to the door. When he opened the door it was October standing there.

"Took you long enough!" She huffed as she pushed past him into the apartment, still acting as if she lived here.

Karl's ex-fiancée was a sewer dwarf from the Battledeep clan named October. October Battledeep was going to the prestigious Malwonkee Technical Institute of Applied Sorcery for their Enchanted Blacksmithing program. While they had been together he had helped her get through a lot of her prerequisite courses at the local community college of magic and summoning. She was determined to be more than just a sewage pipe tinkerer like her father, Drainmeister Agamemnon Battledeep. Even though they had broken up, and even though no other being in the multiverse could send Karl into paroxysms of frustration and anger like she could in under fifteen seconds, they maintained a (more or less) close friendship. The bridge troll she was dating, Bill, was an acquaintance of Karl's who had met October while teaching a remedial divination course (*Tea Leaves, Crystal Balls, and You: Introduction to Divination*) at the community college.

He couldn't really be angry at Bill, he was an all right sort. Sure, he might mug the occasional traveler who passed over his bridge. But that sort of thing is to be expected; Bill is a bridge troll and bridge trolls have a long history of doing this. It is a deeply held familial and cultural tradition. What was important is that Bill treated October with respect and kindness. Still, Karl found it difficult to stomach the two of them together at times. Furthermore, Karl did not envy Bill, for Agamemnon was Bill's problem now. The Drainmeister was a huge ass who refused to speak anything but Gutter Dwarven around Karl. He had never approved of Karl and October's relationship and he was very up front about it. It gave Karl deep sense of satisfaction to think about how October dating a bridge troll was effecting Mr. Battledeep. The sewer dwarves and the bridge trolls had a turbulent history, and Agamemnon Battledeep was a bit of a bigot.

October presented her left hand, "Guess what happened?" she said. Karl could see a simple golden ring around her left ring finger. His heart sank.

"Y-you got *married*?" He said in disbelief.

"Yup. Kinda *had* to."

His mind screeched to a sudden halt. *Oh no.*

"Because I am pregnant."

"Oh. I-I see." Karl was in a daze. Everything started to go grey around the edges and he reached out to lean on something so as not to fall flat on his face. She saw he was teetering and helped him to the couch and sat next to him.

"You okay?" she asked with genuine concern. October was a good person, she was bright and stronger than she gave herself credit for. It was part of why he had been so attracted to her when they met. It was as if in the instant her saw her standing in the used books store, that she had a good heart.

"I-I think I will be. When did this happen?" He was numb.

"Over the weekend. After I found out. You're taking this better than I thought. I figured you'd be angrier." She wore an apologetic, almost sheepish, smile.

"It's been an unsettling week. Getting increasingly more unsettling."

"I thought you'd hate me more than you already do." She looked down with a subtle, pained expression. "I know that I wasn't always kind to you. I could've been a better fiancée."

"We both could've been better to each other. Oh, October, I don't hate you. I have never hated you. I swore an oath to always love you and I do. Even when you frustrated the shit out of me and made me feel horribly alone."

She started to quietly cry. Karl put his arm around her and comforted her. She leaned in and laid her head on his shoulder. "It'll be okay, October. I still love you, Sugarbear. Always."

After a few seconds, she gently pushed him away and regained her composure. "He really *is* wonderful to me."

"I know. That's good. I am glad you have someone." While this was true, it also stung deeply.

Since the breakup Karl had a small string of spectacularly unsuccessful attempts at romance. Finally, he simply accepted that he was one of those people that was meant to be alone. He set his mind to learning to appreciate the loneliness. He had, unsurprisingly, little success in this regard.

"I heard about what happened." She said with a sympathetic wince on her face.

"How?" Karl said, truly taken aback by how fast the news of his firing was getting around.

"It was on the news." October grabbed his remote control and turned the TV on. She found a local news channel (after a few pauses on the tackiest and most gods-awful reality shows).

"...and on a lighter note: remember that *lunatic* who went on and on about some kind of 'UFO encounter' last week? Well, we have an exclusive interview with someone from his previous place of employment. If you love to laugh, watch this." Said the anchor like some kind of brain-dead animatronic Barbie doll.

Then Psycho Joe was on TV in front of the store. There it was live and in living color. Karl was being called a joke, a jerk, a fool, and crazy. PJ made up some kind of cock and bull story about how Karl was let go because of poor performance and lack of motivation, as well as being some kind of sad weirdo on top of that. Then, with a crazed look in his good eye, PJ launched into an unsolicited rant plugging the store. He foamed at the mouth like a deranged carnival barker caught up an in ecstatic fury. As the reporter wrestled the microphone away from him, PJ kept screaming about the low prices on thongs with cartoon characters on them. The reporter finally seized control of the microphone, shoved PJ by the face out of the shot, and signed off. Little Lolo, dressed as his favorite comic book hero (Cardboard and Duct Tape Man) was attempting to drag PJ back into the store.

Great. Karl thought, *how am I supposed to find a new job when everyone thinks I am some kind of jerk?*

"I know you, Karl. I know how hard you worked and how much you loved your job and your customers. I know how mean those guys were to you. I am so sorry this is happening to you." Said October with honest compassion. "If you need anything, please call. We will do our best to help; Bill and I." She got up and made her way out. Karl was speechless and crestfallen. They hugged goodbye and October left.

After a long while of stunned silence, Karl decided to clean himself up and go for a walk. He had no particular destination in mind. He just needed to get away from everything.

He wandered with no thought as to where or when he had to be anywhere. He hadn't done this in a very long time and found it to be agreeable. For a moment Karl felt something like a weight beginning to lift as he felt a rare glimpse of the sun on his face. Karl watched the clouds roll by as he sat on a park bench under a tree. Just as he begin to form the thought that there might be some slim possibility that there could maybe be a silver lining to all of this, something smelly, slimy, and wet hit his face. Hard. Then again on his left shoulder, and again on the left side of his chest. It hit him hard enough to leave a stinging welt. There was uproarious laughter as a group of bugbear children all scurried away in different directions. As they laughed they sung a little rhyme: "Karl the goblin, dumb as a hat pin, can't find a job, because he's got no knob!" The little shits had coated him in rotten tomatoes, runny and rancid yogurt, and moldy chucks of curdled cheese glop. The miniscule terrorists had scattered to the winds, and in the distance the nursery rhyme repeated again and again until it was too far off to hear. It was literally adding insult to injury.

That's it. I need to get the fuck out of this town. Karl resolved as he wiped the disgusting refuse from his face with his kerchief. By this time many of the adults started to laugh as well. Karl saw a constable doubled over with tears streaming down his face, laughing so hard as to have trouble breathing. *Yes, I am quite done here.* Karl knew where he had to go.

One of Karl's best friends was Toby Seven Hills. Toby was a halfling from the Seven Shires Nation Reservation who had fought in The War. They had met many years ago after The War working at *Phipps Odd Emporium and Parlour of the Unusual*. The two of them hit it off instantly after quite an adventure with a cursed tome and a monkey's paw; and that was their first week. Toby was a highly skilled exorcist and made a very comfortable living travelling the galaxy casting out demons and evicting ghosts. Usually for Guild officers and minor merchant houses. (Karl knew there was a joke hidden somewhere in there about the wealthy, exorcists, skeletons, and closets.) Whenever Toby was in town, they'd go out for a steak and some drinks, maybe go to *The Arena* for some sport. *The Arena* being their favorite local cabaret.

Those were halcyon days working for Old Man Phipps. The old fella had a nose for talent and the building of a team. Everyone in the employ of the Old Man was a story unto themselves and genuinely fun to work with; but none so amazing as Phipps himself. Phipps, when the boys knew him, seemed as old as the mountains yet possessed a youthful, even mischievous, gleam in his eye. He was a font of wisdom, dirty limericks, and clever puns. Bartleby J. Phipps was an adventurer and explorer back when the world was largely unexplored. Just after the Great Cataclysm but before The First Contact War. He boldly went into the unknown and recovered lost treasures, rediscovered ancient temple ruins, battled exotic monstrosities, romanced equally exotic women from places both faraway and provincial. *The Old Man* (said with an enduring affection and respect) was never so content than when in the rather impressive library of his study perusing old maps and scrolls, and examining weird talismans and trinkets. Well, except for dinner time. Phipps would have a table set for all his employees to dine at and have discussions, tell jokes, and recall stories old and new. He would sit at the head of that table and take part in all of it. Bartleby would claim that the young folks' company kept him young. It was his *Salon of the Extraordinary*. Bartleby J. Phipps was a rarity: he was a good and generous man who had a smile and a firm hand shake for everyone he met.

Karl knocked at Toby's door with the lingering smell of rotten vegetables and dairy wafting off of him. In moments Toby answered. "*Karl*! What is up, my friend?!" Toby said with a confused smile as he saw the tomato stains on Karl. One of Toby's seven cats whipped by the both of them and bolted into the garden, then another after it in hot pursuit. "*Louie! Mozart!*" shouted a startled Toby in mild frustration. "Yeah, they'll be in the mint. At least they catch a varmint or two. What happened to you? Come in and wash up."

Karl bent down to enter through the smallish, roundish door and closed it behind him. Toby's parents were there for a visit all the way from the Reservation. Then Karl remembered that this was the Harvest Feast, a very important holiday for the halfling peoples. Now, he felt like a royal jerk.

Those many years ago, working at the Emporium, Toby's folks lived with him in the city. Karl was pretty much on his own and spent so much time hanging out with Toby that Toby's parents kind of unofficially adopted him. He had always known them to be kind, gentle people with an abundance of mirth. Toby would laugh when Karl would say as much and reply, "Yeah, well you didn't know them when I was growing up." Eventually they moved back to the Seven Shires Nation; and Toby and Karl were, for a while, roommates.

"Hey, son! How you doing?" Toby's father, Toby Senior, crossed the room to give Karl a hug, followed by Toby's mother.

"We haven't seen you in a long time, honey. How've you been?" She hugged him and gave him a small kiss on the cheek. "You're always welcome and we are glad to have you. This is what the Harvest Feast is for: *family*. Come and eat." Since Karl's mother died, Mrs. Seven Hills took it upon herself to look after him in small ways.

May the halfling harvest saints bless these kind people. They must not watch TV. Thought Karl as he reciprocated the warm welcome he had received. *This would be the only place where I would be welcome, I reckon.*

"I've been... hanging in there. How have you been?" Karl deflected. He felt that it would only burden these wonderful people if they knew what was going on.

"Oh, you know how it is, keeping busy, visiting relatives. We travel for a season and then return home to tend the gardens and ready for winter." Toby Sr. said.

"Let the boy clean up and have a plate, love!" Mrs. Seven Hills gently urged.

"Oh! Yes, of course. Clean up, son, and then come and get some grub. I'll fix you a plate." Said Toby Sr. jovially.

Toby gave him a towel and Karl made his way to the washroom and did his best to scrub off the retched glop. *This shirt is just ruined*! He thought as he looked himself over in the mirror.

Toby was right outside, in the hallway. "So, *kids* did this?"

"Yeah. They even had a very nasty rhyme about me. Toby, I think I am done here. I just don't see a future in this town for me anymore. To be honest, the future I did see, working at Tombstone, didn't appeal that much anyway." Karl scrubbed his face and arms hard, as if he could wash off the sense of humiliation and failure with a bar of soap.

"That is messed up, man. Look, if you're all right with a little travelling, I have a gig coming up and if you'd like to tag along that'd be pretty cool." Toby suggested as they made their way down the hall back to the living room.

"You know, why not? I think that would be perfect, Toby." Karl felt hesitant to give completely into hope. Every time he had done so for the past few days it didn't go well. In any regard, it would be good to get away with a friend. "Where are we headed?"

"The Crumbling Mountains of the Elder Beasts, on New Mars." Answered Toby.

***

Karl had twenty-seven days left to find a job, or be evicted. Toby assured him they would get back by then. "Five days. Tops. I guarantee." He said with the utmost confidence. "Eh, *maybe* seven. But that's it! Probably."

They were at Karl's apartment packing a bag for the trip. Toby was browsing through a pile of books. Karl had many towers of books throughout his dusty apartment. There were books on shelves, books in nooks, books on tables, and even under chairs. The walls of Karl's apartment were adorned with great science fiction movie posters and enlarged reproductions of classic comic book covers. Karl remembered that when he first moved in he was in such a deep state of depression that he didn't unpack his books for six months. It took another six months before he decided to frame and hang his poster collection. Eventually he rebuilt his life piecemeal. He'd find an old, plush, upholstered chair on the street that still had some good years left. Or a neighbor was moving out and abandoned a lovely dresser. Or a friend was buying new kitchenware and unloaded the old stuff on a grateful, newly reinstated, bachelor. Yard sales and second hand stores created the eclectic, well worn, yet cared for, look of Karl's apartment.

"Hey, is that *Bartleby's Bottomless Bag*?" inquired Toby. "Haven't seen that in a while. Not since we had that place together." It resembled a carpet bag with beautiful fractal paisley patterns of deep blue, bright golden hues, and rich coppery rust colors. The patterns appeared to dance hypnotically.

"Yeah. Old Man Phipps left it to me in his will. He said it was the only luggage a body would ever need." Karl was hurriedly searching the apartment looking for any items that might be of use. He had a pile of strange knick knacks next to the bag. Every now and again Karl came across tiny, unusual, treasures that he would squirrel away just in case. Surely, a trip to New Mars was the time to pull these little handy trinkets out of their hiding places if ever there was. In a few hours they would be departing and Karl could not help but be excited, and a little worried. New Mars was a place he had always wanted to visit and he had no idea what to really expect. He hoped that it would live up to his dreams.

"I got *Phipps's Phlogistonickal Penknife*. It's come in quite handy a number of times in my line of work, as you well know." Toby produced the lovely, finely crafted, ifrit horn and mother-of-pearl handled, pen knife that seemed to shiver and gleam in the light. "Ooh. That's odd. It senses danger."

Just then the door crashed open. Splinters flew everywhere and a huge gorilla in a very expensive suit squeezed in through the broken doorframe. He had a silver streak in his hair and a black patch over his right eye. He swaggered into the room, looked at the flabbergasted Karl and Toby, and smiled. He had a golden front tooth with a diamond embedded in it. The smile had an utterly terrifying nature to it. It was cold and suggested a predatory demeanor.

After a long beat, a slender and very well dressed woman seemed to glide through the open doorway. Her long, flowing, silver strands of hair were like an ocean of argent silk with a gentle wave to it. Her eyes were like perfect circles made of incandescent violet gems surrounded by the purest ivory. Her skin was flawless and like smooth gray marble with a hint of bright ocean blue. Her dress was sheer and clingy. It draped past her feet and flowed like delicate tendrils of smoke. Her almond shaped eyes, high cheekbones, and pointed ears declared her elven heritage. Her perfect dispassionate smile and the arrogance that radiated from her like the cold from a dark sun indicated that she was a dark elf. She was beautiful, graceful, and dangerous like a black mamba.

"Greetings, gentlemen." She said, her voice was like the song that lured sailors to their doom; intoxicating and like a talon hooked into the tender sinews of your heart. "I was given to understand that one of you bore witness to a cosmological event recently?"

Karl could hear the upstairs door to Widow Roaches' apartment slam and footfalls stomp down the stairs. From the stairwell Mrs. Roache yelled, "*Maniac*! What is going…?!" As Mrs. Roache turned the corner and stepped into view through the damaged doorway she met the gaze of the dark elven lady and without missing a beat silently crept back upstairs with haste.

"How unpleasant." The strangely alluring woman turned her attention back to Toby and Karl. "Allow me to introduce myself. I am Ariadne Vae, and this ape is my long-time associate, Mr. Damocles Kong." The gorilla barely nodded, his one good eye never seeming to blink. "I understand that one of you is a Mr. Karl Snotwaller?" The diamond-cut perfect smile never slipped.

Her gaze was solidly fixed on Karl and it unnerved him. He understood that the question was rhetorical. It meant that she already knew who he was. "Y-Yes." Karl raised his hand.

Vae started to approach Karl, but Kong interceded. He stepped up, shielding her from the two friends, with his eye locked onto the penknife in Toby's hand.

"Mr. Kong, I assure you, that young Mr. Seven Hills means no harm. He will place the item in his pocket and have a seat, no?" She set her attention on Toby as his hand slowly tightened around his knife. Toby grit his teeth and his whole body seemed as a metal coil, wound tightly and about to snap.

Karl looked over at Toby and with a look asked him to do as she said. Grudgingly, Toby put the penknife away in his pocket and had a seat. Toby was one of the most easy-going and mellow people Karl had ever known, but he knew his friend was capable of transforming in the blink of an eye. It was his training as a soldier; experiences that would forever be a part of him. They had faced dangers together before, and Karl both recognized his friends' subtle shifts in mood and he knew how to effectively and directly communicate to his friend in spite of the clouding effect these episodes had on Toby's rational mind. But, most of the time, when the chips were down, Karl welcomed Toby's ability to respond to threats with an absolute fearlessness and an iron resolve to bend all foes into submission or break them into dust.

"You see, Mr. Kong? Young Mr. Seven Hills has shown incredible resolve, exemplary good manners, and a keen intellect. Shall we not reciprocate?" Kong snorted out a hard, hot, gust of air and stepped down. "Forgive me, gentlemen, but I shall remain standing." She said with the uncanny grace of an ethereal ballerina.

"I mean you no harm, Mr. Snotwaller. In point of fact, I am here to bring you an offer." She gestured to Kong and he removed the black, leather driving glove from his right hand. Underneath was a mechanical hand made of metal. He outstretched his arm and held his hand palm-side up. The hand itself split open along nearly invisible seams, revealing clockworks, gears, and strange lights inside. They shifted and reformed into what appeared to be three gyroscope-like frameworks that held lenses spinning inside them. Three tight, bright, beams of light came from what was once his palm and were focused and refracted through the spinning lenses. The beams started to pulsate with incredibly rapid patterns so fast the eye could barely detect them. A static-filled hiss sharpened into a voice as the light from the dervish lenses were recollected into a perfect three-dimensional image.

A hooded figure floated above Kong's mechanical hand. "Mr. Snotwaller. You may address me as Mr. Blackdagger. I know you were contacted recently by a being calling itself *The High Archon*. I am prepared to offer you a substantial amount of money for a moment of your time. You will never have to worry about your debts, or where your next meal is coming from, or where you will lay your head at night. Nor will you be forced to work for an ungrateful lout incapable of appreciating your meritorious qualities ever again. You will be your own master. Furthermore, you will be in a position to help those you care for; to elevate them as well from worry over financial hardships. All you have to do is tell me what the High Archon told you. That is all, and then you will never be contacted or bothered again." The hooded figure waited for a reply.

"M-Mr. Blackdagger, sir. I appreciate the offer, and I really wish I could take it, but, honestly, I just don't remember what the ball of fire said... Sir." Karl said as deferentially as possible.

"Mr. Snotwaller, do not be mistaken, this is the first, last, and *only* offer I shall make." The hooded figure's aura seemed to shift as if to drive home intent.

"Sir, all I can remember was it saying something about something being some sort of destiny. My destiny. I truly can't help you more."

"I see. You think what it imparted to you is important enough to maintain the confidence of an alien being? To place yourself in such danger out of a misguided sense of duty and honor... I can almost respect that. Foolish as it is. Sleep on it, Mr. Snotwaller. Consider my offer. Henceforth, you shall deal with Ms. Vae. Good day." The image zipped out of existence and Kong's mechanical hand quickly whizzed and ratcheted back into its original shape. Kong replaced the glove and stood, staring at the two friends with a disconcerting intensity.

"Good day, gentlemen. Please accept this gift from Mr. Blackdagger for you time today. He hopes it illustrates the veracity of his offer." Said Vae coolly, yet cordially. Kong removed a thick envelope from inside his overcoat pocket and tossed it onto the, slightly scratched, wagon wheel coffee table. "Please, remain comfortably seated, gentlemen. We will show ourselves out." Damocles Kong and Ariadne Vae stepped out into the hallway over the broken fragments of what used to be Karl's front door. Vae turned and said, "Good day, Mr. Seven Hills, Mr. Snotwaller. I shall be in touch." She then made a swanlike flourishing gesture with her hand and followed that with a sharp snap of her fingers. Just before she snapped her fingers she said with authority, *"Reparare in januis!"*

The once kicked-down door rose up and reformed with all of its scattered pieces into a whole door. It then clapped back into its doorframe and aligned itself with similarly reforming hinges. The whole thing looked good as new within the breadth of a single second.

Though they could not see it, a single blood tear fell from the corner of Ariadne Vae's left eye. All magic takes a toll. To circumvent the so-called laws of the universe, to ruffle the smooth fabric of reality, it costs a sliver of yourself. It is why most sensible magicians take time to perform proper protective rituals and meditative practices. These lengthy rituals are laid down in centuries-old, tried-and-true, formulae written in dusty grimoires handed down from master to apprentice. Magic-users work in covens or guilds so as to share the load and pool knowledge and experience. They prefer to operate in places of high natural mystical significance at times of astrological conjunction in order to take advantage of natural "high tides" in the universe's fields of energy. Clever casters would entreat spiritual entities to assist in the casting of spells with litanies of arguments and proofs as to why the assistance was in their best interests. They utilize reagents (like unicorn horns, phoenix feathers, dragon teeth, and faerie wings) as vessels of natural energies to exchange in lieu of their own life forces. Lists of effective reagents (and their possible side-effects) are catalogued in great detail in the spell formulas within the afore-mentioned grimoires. Even simple magical effects can fatigue a trained caster. In time, with rest, he or she recovers the spent energy; but magic so swift, so blatant, and so powerful as to completely recreate something from its destroyed components has a dire cost. Real magic, while capable by anyone with a book and some spare time, was uncommon because of the costs; either in long hours of study and practice, or in blood. She dabbed the bloody teardrop away with a deeply, almost velvety, scarlet silk handkerchief that seemed to drink the sanguine bead into it. At no time did her perfect composure ever slip.

Karl and Toby looked at the envelope the two visitors had left behind. This was an unexpected turn of events.

***

The trip to New Mars was extremely pleasant. Toby's mysterious client had paid for deluxe accommodations. The friends shared a luxury suite to themselves. The room had an outstanding view of the cosmos as they sailed through space. The ship resembled a gigantic fan tailed goldfish that oscillated in the full spectrum of colors as light danced off its opalescent scales. Its massive streaming tailfins, easily twice-over the length of the fish-ship itself, rhythmically swayed as it propelled itself through the void. The ships structure, crew areas, passenger accommodations, as well as the cargo spaces, were grown out of the head of the epic spacefaring fish. It was a living ship crafted by an elite cadre of elven archmages known as *the Shipwrights*. Their living ships were works of art and this one was absolutely one of the most beautiful things Karl had ever seen. The ship was named *Sojourn* and its consciousness infused every inch the ship.

The leviathanesque creature was psychically linked with the ship's captain, a lovely four-armed woman named Marzipan P. Jones, in a symbiotic relationship. Captain Jones was an excellent specimen of physical fitness and rugged beauty. Her olive complected skin was a complexly intertwined tapestry of battle scars and beautifully vivid tattoos. Her hair was cut in the Mohawk fashion and dyed the brilliant colors of a rainbow-hued tropical bird. Her smokey eyes, like two deep amber pools of dark honey, were at the heart of her large, honest smiles. Her laugh was boisterous, genuine, and infectious. Yet, always she remained vigilant and lucid. She bore the weight of her responsibilities with an easy charm and affability. Not only was she, as captain of this vessel, responsible for the comfort, but also the safety of the crew and passengers. Marzipan, daughter of Professor Archimedes Jones, was an expert pistoleer and wore four six-guns at all times. She would host demonstrations of her unique gift for marksmanship regularly throughout the journey to entertain her guests, but also as a clear message to those who had inclinations towards troublemaking that they should earnestly revisit that intent. At dinner, she would regale everyone at the table with stories of adventure and intrigue, sometimes a bit bawdier than some dinner guests were used to, but easily forgiven within the wink of an eye from the fair captain. She did not shy from telling the stories behind each of her scars, and what's more is that anyone she would share the tales with would remain riveted for the entire story and the next. Across her back, from shoulder to shoulder, was an elaborately illustrated tattooed banner of bone whites, bright sky blues, and fiery reds, upon which was written a quote from antiquity by Samuel Clemens: *"The report of my death was an exaggeration."* Also, once, she played two banjoes at the same time. It was very impressive.

The meals were exquisite and far richer than the two were used to. Toby declared gleefully that a fellow could become used to fine dining. Karl simply appreciated the experience, for he knew better than most that good things are fleeting in this life. Karl opened up his senses to take in everything around him. The feel of the leather on the couches in the lounge was cool and soft. One felt as if they couldn't tell where their body ended and the couch began as they sank into its pillowy cushions. The faint, yet definite, aroma of fresh baked vanilla and cinnamon apples infused the room. When Karl asked Captain Jones about the wonderful aroma, she said that it was a psionic side effect of Sojourn monitoring the health of each passenger. If one were to encounter a strong smell of something unpleasant, then they should immediately report to the ships' doctor. (Flatulence was discouraged for obvious reasons.) Everyone smelled something equally nice but distinct to themselves. For some it was honeysuckle blossoms and sweet lemonade on a lazy summer afternoon. For others it was the scent of the clean, crisp, coastal air in a garden just after a spring rain. For Toby it was fresh brewed coffee and the smell of bacon cooked to perfection on a cold winter's morning with undertones of peppermint and fir tree.

Karl took special notice of the beautiful ambient music throughout the ship. During conversation with another guest he discovered that the music itself was in actuality Sojourn's voice. It bore an amazing resemblance to a classical string quartet: the velvety rumble of the bass cello, the entrancing seductive violin, the viola's sultry tones, and the rich and emotive sounds of the clarinet. While Sojourn's voice can easily communicate her emotional state, only Captain Jones through her symbiotic link (or a member of the elusive and mythic Shipwrights) could fully understand the complex nature of the living ship's language. It consists of four blended streams of thoughts, concepts, and emotions playing in harmony using musical phrases and mathematics to communicate ideas in a profoundly nuanced and complete manner. Sometimes Sojourn, being linked to Captain Jones, created a kind of living soundtrack for her moods, providing mood music when she told one of her amazing stories.

Sojourn would dip into the atmospheres of alien worlds to give the passengers a safe glimpse of exotic places whose awesome beauty paralleled the swift lethality of their surfaces. Through the strange gases on theses planets the nebulae clouds and star fields seems to glimmer brighter from the forward observatory. It was through Karl's openness to wonder that Toby gained renewed appreciation for the world around him. It's what made Karl such an excellent companion on a trip like this. Being an exorcist was like being a soldier: both were hard callings that would take a hefty fee from one's soul. It is through wonder that souls may heal and grow.

The ships amazing arboretum, in addition to being a wonderfully manicured and colorful area for relaxation and recreation, was also vital to atmospheric processing, water reclamation, and food production on board Sojourn. When Karl wanted to be by himself and reflect on the events that had transpired as of late, he would come here and feel somehow connected to something greater. Of course, a tiny, covert, bit of Toby's pipe weed also helped. The ship also hosted a public dining room that could be converted for parties and weddings, a small movie theatre, a game room and bar with stage for live performers, and a gymnasium complete with swimming pool, track, and courts for multiple sports. Karl made sure to try a little bit of everything. He had decided that if this Mr. Blackdagger were real, then this whole High Archon thing must also be real. It was here in the garden that he realized that if he wanted to actually find out what his destiny was supposed to be, that he had better learn to say *"yes"* to what life places in front of him instead of *"no."*

Up until two days ago, I didn't even know that that fiery-boomy-thing even *had* a name. He thought as he sat alone and felt Sojourn's garden atmospheric regulation system (*or G.A.R.S.*) at work in the gentle flower-scented breeze that caressed his face. His reverie was interrupted by the captain's seneschal, valet, first mate, and body guard; a taciturn and stoic minotaur whom Captain Jones called Mr. Tor.

Karl attempted to snuff out the smoldering pipe. "Erh... um... this is *medicinal*. I have a prescription. L- Let me see where I left it." Karl pretended to pat down his pockets in search of the nonexistent prescription.

Mr. Tor handed an envelope to Karl and said in an indifferent, baritone voice, "This just arrived over the ships secure channel."

"S-secure channel? Oh. Okay." Said Karl slowly becoming more away of what that meant. Karl took the envelope from Mr. Tor.

"The captain would like a word with you at your earliest convenience." With that the hulking man-beast turned and left Karl to himself in the gardens.

ATTN: MR KARL SNOTWALLER

RE: MR BLACKDAGGERS OFFER. ANSWER REQUIRED UPON RETURN ARRIVAL. WILL CONTACT YOU.

BEST REGARDS.

A.V.

This certainly sends the message home. Karl let out a heavy sigh and got himself up and out of the gardens. Not even the sublime tranquility here could break down the anxiety that this correspondence brought out. He returned to the suite in search of

Toby to inform him of this new wrinkle. Who he found, however, was Captain Jones. She was waiting alone for him in the suite. Her normally warm face now made into a severe mask by necessities of her position as protector of this ship and all souls aboard.

"Mr. Snotwaller, what do you know about Aris Blackdagger?" she rose from her seated position and stood, arms crossed, facing Karl.

"Until *this* very moment, I didn't know he had a first name other than Mister." Responded Karl, still a little under the effects of the halfling pipe weed.

That broke through the Captain's defenses and she cracked a smile. "May I call you 'Karl', Karl? Aris Blackdagger is a very dangerous man. But, I've got a hunch that you are good people. You don't want to harm this ship or the people on it, do you Karl?"

"Oh, no! Not at all! I've truly enjoyed my time on Sojourn, Captain Jones. It's been just *amazing*. All the things I have seen and done. I feel something inside, like butterflies. It's nice."

With a look of one part relief and one part amusement, she said, "Karl, I am glad you like it here. Feel free to call me Marz. I will see you later at dinner." She crossed the room and made her way to the door. She turned and added, "Oh, and one more thing: we are in interstellar space, Karl. There are no laws here regarding the consumption of herbal remedies. But, please be aware of the no smoking areas. They are noted for everyone's safety and enjoyment." With a wink and a smile she showed herself out. There was *something* about her... you just never quite knew if she was flirting.

***

The customs agents were especially thorough in Corona, the capital city of New Mars. There were long lines at the spaceport to have bags examined and when contraband was found, the traveler was "*quarantined*" for weeks sometimes (pending a ruling from the Office of Health and Interstellar Transportation). Once cleared, however, then the real fun begins. The traveler is then charged with anything from smuggling, to tax evasion, to failure to obey official signage, to improper footwear in a loading zone. Whatever the Department of

Interstellar Commerce and Safety can make stick. Most were found guilty and either had to pay steep fines or were incarcerated. Usually both.

The supernatural nature of Karl's luggage ensured that it was beyond suspicion at all times. Just something about its swirling, hypnotic design, which simply made it very hard to believe anything bad could be inside of it. No sir, this bag was fine. No need to bother searching that. Just a boring old bag. Old Man Phipps had done quite a bit of smuggling in his youth. Usually herbal remedies, but sometimes rare books, or ancient artifacts. And it wasn't only useful for circumventing attention from commerce or antiquities officials, the bag had saved more than a few priceless treasures from highwaymen and pirates. Once, it helped young Phipps sneak a beloved pet past an evil ex-girlfriend.

Toby held licenses and certifications to practice in numerous principalities and nations. Additionally, many of these also granted the right to carry weapons and/or transport unusual and exotic cargo in the course of performing his duties for the state or private client. The officials hardly batted an eye at the penknife and treated Toby's baggage with great care, lest they set loose something that could melt their faces off.

"They sent a car for us." Toby informed Karl.

"I think I can see it." Said Karl as he helped Toby push a luggage cart. "There." Karl pointed. "The squiddish fellow in the *driver's* uniform. No, over *there*, with the bored expression. He's got a sign."

In front of a long, sleek, silver car that resembled a highly stylized and aerodynamic floating stingray, seemingly made of liquid metal, there stood a tentacle-faced humanoid in a black suit. It held up a sign that read "*Mr. Seven Hills and Guest.*" Its bulbous kaleidoscope eyes swiveled forward in the same direction facing them. The driver's skin color changed to a rapidly alternating pattern bright purple and red flashes when it saw Karl and Toby. It put the sign away and approached them.

"How do you know he's bored?" asked Toby.

"No idea, he could be ecstatic for all I know. I only took two semesters of Squiddish in art school. Squiddish faces are *very* hard to read. All tentacles really." Replied Karl.

It stopped in front of them and nodded politely. It communicated through gestures and rapid pigment changes that it would be happy to take the cart from them and load their baggage aboard the vehicle. It pushed the cart up to the sky car and opened the door for them to take a seat in the back. It then shut the door after them and began to load up the car.

The gleaming vehicle was phenomenally fast and maneuverable. It slipped through traffic and swiftly past other sky cars like an arrow loosed from an archer's bow with naught but a whisper as it passed. Inside the car, Karl watched the city speed by like a movie stuck in fast forward through his passenger window. He held fast to his bag, having declined to surrender it to the driver. The recent message from Mr. Blackdagger had set him on edge. Toby grabbed a can of soda from the minibar, popped its top with a crunch-hiss, and then produced a half-finished bag of snacks from seemingly nowhere. Toby offered Karl some, but Karl had no appetite.

"Karl, you've got nothing to worry about. One: we've been in situations worse than what appears to be a very nice car ride to see a very wealthy potential client of mine. Two: the whole Blackdagger thing is apparently on hold until you get home. Which you don't even *have to* be for like twenty days yet (more or less) in order to deal with your landlady. Three: you are actually *on* New Mars, man! So, cheer up! I'll knock this out and we will have a few days to explore this place." reassured Toby. As an afterthought, he added, "Do you know if they have an Arena here?"

"I think I saw one back near the spaceport." Replied Karl, lost in thought. "Pretty sure the cover charge is the same."

The sky car made its way to a palatial manor just outside of the sprawling megalopolis of Corona, nestled in the Uncanny Valley at the foot of the Crumbling Mountains of the Elder Beasts. The mountains were beyond anything that Karl had imagined. He had seen pictures and watched movies, but to see them in person was truly awe inspiring. For a moment, when he set his eyes upon them for the first time, their sheer majesty took him away from every single problem that had him in a vice grip since he left Sojourn. Somehow, Karl knew that he was supposed to be here. Yes, there are sights so full of beauty, majesty, and awe that the eyes cannot possibly take it all in, and out of necessity of the soul, one's heart must to grow just a bit bigger to do so.

There is a small, still voice deep inside each of us. In the din and cacophony of modern life and the scramble for survival, it is exceedingly easy to miss that voice amidst the chaos and compromise. Eventually, if you have to keep scrambling long enough, you forget it ever existed. You just go along in life forgetting a little more with each tired and rote step who you even were. One day you look in the mirror and don't have a clue who is looking back. How could you have strayed so far from your dreams? Sights like the mountains here, they cut right through the noise and reach the truest self, deep inside. It's like returning home after being lost for a very long time.

The two were escorted through the singularly opulent manor to a library in its west wing. There a slim, feline metahuman gentleman waited. He was seated behind a large oak desk going through a veritable mountain of books as if in the middle of a desperate search. When Toby and Karl entered, he removed his wire-framed glasses, stood up and came from behind the desk to meet them. He was dressed impeccably in the finest suit Karl had ever seen. The material seemed to be preternatural, like a suit made of the very stuff of night itself.

The slim gentleman greeted them. "Mr. Seven Hills, thank you for coming. I trust your journey was pleasant?" He shook Toby's hand. "I see you have brought an *assistant*?"

"This is Karl Snotwaller. A fellow professional I brought in as a, let's just say, *consultant*. He's kind of an expert on xenocryptodaemonology." Toby had a gift for not exactly lying by bending words in just the perfect way.

Karl shook the man's hand in surprised silence and gave the feline gentleman a silent nod hello while wearing a mildly uncomfortable and completely unprepared look on his face.

"Hello, Mr. Snotwaller. It's a pleasure to meet you. I trust that I can count on your confidentiality, as I can Mr. Seven Hills'?"

"Er, um, I mean, yes. O-Of course!" coughed out Karl. "Excuse me, do you have any water?" As soon as the question was asked a clockwork servant made of polished brass and mahogany varnished to a smooth, rich shine whooshed up to Karl with a tall glass of cool water. "Oh! T-thank you." Said a startled Karl. The mechanical and obsequious valet made a short pleasant whistle from its steam exhaust, followed by a brief, yet somehow chipper, clicking whir from its inner gear works. Karl took the water and the automaton went back to its obfuscated position in the corner with barely a whispering hum from its well-engineered workings.

"Excuse my poor manners in not introducing myself earlier. I am Icarian Phaedra IV. My great grandfather, the first Icarian Phaedra, claimed and established the New Mars Colony nearly two centuries ago. I am his direct descendant and sole inheritor of the entire planet of New Mars."

Karl's jaw dropped a little. He quickly recovered and took a long sip from his water. *Hmm*, he thought, *it even has a little slice of lemon just how I like it. Also, I am going to strangle Toby when we get out of here. Just a tiny bit.*

"In turn, my grandfather and father each took the reins, in their own time. My predecessors turned a frontier colony into a center of commerce, industry, art, and politics. This did not come cheaply or without struggle. There is a cost for success. I suppose it demands a certain ruthlessness." Icarian Phaedra paused, took a deep breath as if to steel himself, and continued. "Faustian deals were made. An extra-dimensional entity demanded payment as per the terms of a blood-contract and I reneged. I need you to help me. You come highly recommended, Mr. Seven Hills. Highly reputable sources say you are the best."

"Mr. Phaedra, I recommend you find yourself a good lawyer specialized in infernal contracts, not an exorcist. I'm sorry, I cannot help you. I bid you a good day and we will see ourselves out." Toby turned to Karl and said, "Come on, Karl. I'm sorry I wasted your time. Let's go."

"Mr. Seven Hills, *please*! I can double my previous offer."

"Mr. Phaedra, you can keep your money. It was your own stupidity and greed that landed you in this trouble. I cannot save you from you. Thank you for the passage here, and good day."

"It was my *great grandfather's* greed, actually, Mr. Seven Hills." Corrected Mr. Phaedra quickly. He cleared his throat and explained, "As I discovered only too late. It was he who struck the accursed bargain. That is the family secret. That is how New Mars was founded and how it flourished. If that deal is broken, New Mars will most likely fall into ruin. The PhaedraCorp Empire will be torn apart by my competitors. But, there are things that matter more than money. The safety, love, and trust of my daughter is worth a thousand worlds." His composure was beginning to fade. "It has my daughter, Mr. Seven Hills. She is the last heir to our title and fortune. *She is only a child.*" With this, Icarian Phaedra's professional and polished demeanor broke down and he wept.

Toby couldn't leave an innocent to suffer and die. He turned back and said, "The job will be very dangerous because this demon came in through the front door. I will need you to do exactly as I say and assist me with any resources I might require. *No questions asked.*"

Mr. Phaedra nodded in agreement as he was no longer capable of speech.

***

Once outside and out of the earshot of Mr. Phaedra, or anyone in his employ, Karl turned to Toby and said, "*Consultant*?! *Expert*?! In *xenocryptodaemonology*?! What in the nine hells was *that* about?" Karl was doing his best to keep his voice low, but everything seemed to be half-growled through a forced smile of gritted teeth.

"You are a professional, you possess a profession. Maybe it's not exorcist *necessarily*, but you earned money for skilled work. And I am consulting you, so you, *technically*, are a consultant. Even a novice possesses a kind of expertise, just not a very well-polished one. But, I know you are an expert in lots of things; just maybe not things relating to *this* case. Oh, and 'xenocryptodaemonology' is the study of previously unknown, or previously though mythical, alien malevolent spirits... I *think*. And if we are being totally honest here, that is a mighty big umbrella. I mean, that could be pretty much anything you'll encounter on this gig when you think about it. So, I was being honest. Mostly.

"Anyway, Karl, you know I have always said you'd be great at this. You know more about hunting demons that half the guys I know who are actually licensed to do it. You can do this." Toby gave Karl a big reassuring pat on the back. "Besides back in the day, when we both started out working for Mr. Phipps, we had lots of adventures. Those turned out just fine."

"Okay, yeah, but this is some very serious stuff, Toby."

Toby stopped, turned, and looked Karl in the eye. "Karl, I wouldn't have brought you here if I felt you couldn't handle it. I am proud of you, man. On this trip you've come a long way. You've really started to take some first steps towards grabbing life by the balls and giving it a twist for a change. *You are better than how you allow shitty people to treat you.* I want you to remember that." He gave his friend a hug and after three firm pats on the back pulled away and said, "Now let's go kick some demon ass, all right?"

***

Investigators in the employ of Mr. Phaedra had tracked the girl's location to a long abandoned and forgotten temple complex that had been built within the Crumbling Mountains of the Elder Beasts by some precursor proto-dwarf species that faded into extinction eons ago. The temple was carved from the solid mountainside and was filled with ingenious ancient traps and ferocious beasts that had taken up residence since the original owners vanished long ago.

A team of researchers and specialists had been sent to these ruins nearly eighty years before. It was supposed to be a study of the unique archeological find, but no one ever returned. Records exist of early radio communications of the research team having established an initial base camp upon reaching the entrance to the ruins. Then nothing. Rescue teams found no trace of them. No camp site, no equipment, no bodies, nothing; it was as if they had never existed.

A rugged looking sky truck bearing the PhaedraCorp Security logo broke through the clouds below and unloaded Karl and Toby at the snowy plateau where the research team vanished two decades before. The air was much thinner up here than Karl was used to. Fortunately, Toby had an ample supply of *Zephyr's Alchemical Aerosol Elixir Inhalers* to deal with the problems of thin air or miasma. Karl took a puff and instantly the fatigue lifted and the edges of his vision returned from a gray fog. A burly chap in a maroon PhaedraCorp Security uniform heaved out camping gear and supplies. Included in the supplies was a cryogenic stasis pod, three kegs of holy water, two dozen each of Colloidal Silver Tear Gas grenades and UV Flash-Bang grenades. Finally, a large and very expensive radio-transmitter-and-receiver-automaton known as *Songbird* was unloaded. Its rugged padded exterior, when collapsed, resembled a cube about a yard on each side made of some kind of hyper strong polymer cast. It easily handled the rough treatment from Mr. Phaedra's personal army. Icarian Phaedra IV lived, for all intents and purposes, as an emperor. Though the empire may fly its flag over New Mars, PhaedraCorp had branches on every world in the empire and beyond. Its corporate logo rose easily twice as high as any banner and blazed brightly over them all day and night.

"This demon must have its origins here." Said Toby, wrapped inside a heavy coat and scarf as the icy wind disheveled his thinning hair. The snow made a soft crunch with each step of his winter boots. "I will have to access every bit of information regarding the peoples who inhabited New Mars before colonization."

The box designated as Songbird let out a soft, pleasant ding, like a clear silver bell rung in response to a correct answer. It started to rattle and shimmy back and forth, and then bounce and nudge itself over and over until the words *"This end up"* and *"Stand clear for deployment"* were visible on its top side. Then, with a soft crack and a hiss of steam escaping, it hatched open and unfolded itself from its boxy shell. What rose from a seated fetal position was a supple and lithe automaton that had the form of a pulchritudinous clockwork female.

Her eyes opened and she said in a soothingly lyrical, yet simulated, voice, "Mr. Seven Hills, I can recall the entire library of the top three New Martian universities on the matters of paleo-psychology and exo-archeology. In addition I can, if you require, recite verbatim all personal journals, published theses, profiles, and interviews with any and all members of the initial survey team and/or rescue team in regards to the *Precursor Temple Project*. I am a prototype designed by Mr. Icarian Phaedra IV and assembled by the Research and Design Division of PhaedraCorp Automatronics. I am Songbird, and I would be happy to assist you in any way possible."

Karl wasn't sure how to feel. She was beautiful, but not real. She seemed to possess sentience and sapience, but that had to be some very sophisticated programming because automatons weren't people. They didn't feel or want. They were programmed to be obsequious and diligent. While Songbird was all that an automaton should be, Karl could not dismiss the very strong impression that she was clearly exceptional. It made him... *queasy*?

"This is *definitely* more like it!" Toby gave a short hoot and asked Songbird to "Spill the beans, already."

***

The official historical record states that Icarian Phaedra (the First) discovered the arid, red world that would be called New Mars on a routine scan as a captain aboard the small mining vessel, *El Dorado*. He had just started an independent prospecting company, which would later evolve into PhaedraCorp, and this was its first big break in the vast Unexplored Territories. He could never have known that within ninety-six hours of finding this planet that he would be the only survivor of the crew of forty-two.

From orbit, the entrepreneurial captain would find that this planet had unimaginably huge amounts of natural mineral resources. Something the long range scans had somehow missed completely. His official claim was filed before even landing here, with the Office of the Secretary General of Imperial Exploration, nearly one hundred and ninety-seven years prior to Karl and Toby setting foot on the snowy plateau. The experience would be a harrowing and apparently a transformative one for Icarian, for soon afterwards he began to build what would become his corporate empire.

Upon entering the atmosphere, a freak storm came from nowhere and slammed the small ship off course. As the pilot struggled to regain control, it spun wildly into a wooded area. The ship careened into gigantic trees, hundreds of meters tall, and then with great force slammed into the ground. The first crew member to be lost, a ship's hand named Lawrence Bertram died during crash landing. He was crushed by loose cargo when some rigging snapped during the turbulence. He was 22 years old. After the rough landing, the ship's chief mechanic surveyed the damage and felt he could make adequate repairs in a timely manner with the assistance of his team. Two hours into repairs the team was attacked by some kind of huge spider-like predators that operated with viciously efficient pack tactics. The entire eight-person engineering team was killed. The chief mechanic was dragged off screaming. His desiccated body was found the next morning, wrapped in silky strands of webbing.

The medical officer dragged in the body and performed an autopsy to learn more about the creatures and see if an effective defense could be made. He was infected by the tiny parasitic young the monsters had laid inside the corpse of the chief mechanic. As infant "spider" larvae ate away at his brain he went mad and murdered two other members of the crew before vaporizing himself.

It was decided, that with over a quarter of the ship's crew dead and no way to effectively repair the ship, that the survivors could not stay put. The radios weren't working and the ship was caught in a vast forest-wide network of webbing; it was believed that the monsters would return soon to take more victims. The communications officer jury rigged a flame thrower, they remaining crew gathered any food or medical supplies that could be carried, any weapons and ammunition on board, and they set out to escape the Webbed Forest.

Of the surviving thirty, six had injuries that prevented them from travelling. A nurse volunteered to stay behind and care for them until a rescue party arrived. All hopes were pinned on the remaining twenty-three crew members, including the captain, Icarian Phaedra. Over the following days, as they cut and fought their way out of the web, seven were killed by spider-things, one from injuries related to the crash that were more serious than initially surmised, two from the jury-rigged flame thrower exploding in an act of self-sacrifice to allow the rest to get away, two from friendly fire during an attack from the spider-things, and three from an unknown illness that befell them from eating indigenous berries.

By the time they got out of the spider-infested forest, ten ragged and exhausted crewmen remained to reach the foot of a vast mountain range. On the climb up, five fell to their deaths as an avalanche took them all strung together for safety, three died from exposure, and one committed suicide.

While wandering, alone and lost on the planet's surface, in the region that would be later named the Crumbling Mountains of the Elder Beasts, Icarian discovered the ruins of an ancient and bygone civilization. His official journal states that he was attempting to climb to a higher altitude to break free of a strange jamming field that prevented his communications equipment from functioning. He had been trying for days to get a distress signal out so that he might be rescued. He recorded that almost as soon as he found the temple, he was able to get a signal out. With only his flashlight, some rope, and his personal distress beacon, he entered the temple.

Inside the ruins, Icarian discovered highly complex, hauntingly beautiful, yet subtly disturbing religious iconography. He suspected that a species of highly intelligent humanoids must have evolved here and vanished into extinction millennia ago. From their depictions in the stone, he hypothesized that they must have been a type of proto-dwarf. Short, broad, subterranean, and with highly developed engineering, mathematics, and astronomy. They were a war-like people who seemed to worship a pantheon of underworld spirits and practiced horrific sacrificial rites. By the only light to have touched these ruins in countless centuries, he explored the temple.

There was a point where he started to feel as if he was not alone; as if he was being watched. He called out but heard only his own frightened echoing voice. Then, the light from his flashlight sputtered and blinked out. He felt the temperature in the air drop sharply and his hair stood on end. He couldn't see his hand in front of his face and yet he felt a distinct presence in the chamber. It radiated an ancient hatred. He became absolutely certain that whatever he was feeling meant that he shouldn't be in here. He turned to run. Then nothing. Blackness.

Three days later an Imperial Exploratory First Response Search and Rescue team found him just outside of the temple. He seemed fine. Better than fine considering the ordeal he had been through. After a brief and satisfactory examination by the ship's chief medical officer on board the Imperial Exploratory Ship *Vanguard*, he was cleared and returned to civilization. The chief medical officer made note in his official records that Icarian Phaedra was a remarkably fit individual possessing indomitable mental fortitude and the remarkably astounding endurance of a man half his age. The *IES Vanguard* delivered him to the nearest frontier trading post three systems away.

Those injured left behind and the nurse who stayed with them were discovered later, all dead. Killed and eaten by the spider-things. Their skulls had burst open as the hatchlings were birthed from their corpses. The Webbed Forest was firebombed from orbit. Corona was built on its ashes. The creatures that killed the crew were hunted to extinction.

He never spoke of, nor recorded in any way, what happened inside the temple over those three days.

✦✦✦

Songbird explained to Toby in great detail the theories put forward by scholars regarding the Ancients, as the extinct indigenous proto-dwarven people were called. She gave the official historical account of Icarian Phaedra the First's discovery of the ruins.

He then, with the focus of a diamond-cutter, scrutinized the entrance way to the temple. There was faded writing inscribed into the stone around the entrance. He consulted Songbird as to its possible meaning. "I can only extrapolate a working theory utilizing compiled data from the Universities' xeno-linguistics departments, but I can have a rough translation for you momentarily, sir." As Toby started to make notes and sketches about the exterior of the temple in his journal, Karl saw something alarming.

Toby and Songbird were entirely fixated on reading the strange glyphs at the entrance, so Karl found a spot that wasn't covered in snow and had a seat. He opened up his bag and removed from it his cherished pipe. Karl had won the pipe at a card game aboard Sojourn. The previous owner had said that it once belonged to a wizard of some renown. When Karl expressed disbelief, the strange little fellow demonstrated the simple and useful magic infused into the pipe. The beady-eyed, potato-like, mole-man held the long slender pipe, placed its stem to his lips, and inhaled sharply. Karl was delighted to see the wondrous item ignite itself automatically. It was the best hand of cards Karl had ever played. Right about now he figured his frayed nerves could use a little herbal remedy.

Karl's recreational break was cut short by a massive bestial hand coming up over the edge of the snowy plateau and once it found a solid grip the rest of this thing rose up after it. A large ape-like thing with brilliant white fur and shaggy mane pulled itself up to the plateau. Its nostrils were flared, its fierce blue eyes were wide and darting between Karl and his companions, and its odor was the awful smell of flesh putrefying. Once it was settled upon the plateau, it exhaled sharply sending out tendrils of its hot steaming breath and exposed its large yellowed fangs. Its eyes narrowed to angry bright blue coals and settle on the nearest target: Karl. This thing let out a bellowing roar that Karl felt rumble through him.

Toby dropped his journal into the snow and in a flash produced the penknife. With a flick of his wrist the knife opened and then, with an audible pop and a bright spark, a long flaming blade extended out from its hilt. The sudden flare of the fiery blade drew the violent attention of the beast. But, even as the towering yeti turned to face its new foe, Toby was running in full sprint at the shaggy snow creature. With a blood curdling battle cry, Toby, like a fierce little cannon ball, bounded up into the air and came down on the yeti, flaming blade first. The fiery sword sank deep into the beast's breast and it let out an agonizing howl. Toby hung from the weapon's hilt dragging it downward, slicing into the monster's sinewy flesh. The yeti slapped at Toby and he flew all the way back to the temple entrance. He hit the snowy steps of the temple and tumbled to a very still stop. The flaming sword extinguished when the stunned Toby involuntarily released his grip on it. It fell into the snowy plateau and sank with a soft hiss into the ice. Karl's heart seized at the sight of his best friend laying in the snow, still as death.

Enraged, Karl rose up with bag in hand. From the rock he was perched on, he hopped onto the yeti's back. With one hand finding purchase, gripping its thick mane, the other had the magic bag firmly by its handle. He didn't think, he just slipped opening of the bag over the yeti's head. The magical bag seemed to open wider like a snake dislocating its jaws to take in prey. The yeti's entire head was inside the bag and for what seemed like the longest few seconds in all of Karl's life the monster attempted to snatch him off of its back. Then, without warning, the yeti seized up and toppled like a domino into the snow face first. Karl slowly disentangled himself from the monster's fur and ran over to where Toby fell.

Karl turned Toby over. His head hung at a horrific angle. There was shallow breath and his heart beat was thready. "Songbird! Quickly please, get my bag!"

She retrieved the bag from the yeti's head. Its eyes were bloody and its swollen tongue hung out of blue lips frozen in a deathly grimace. Karl dug through his bag until he produced a small pine pencil box. He flipped its latch up and opened it. Inside was a single feather. It radiated brilliant yellows, reds, and oranges Every now and again a cool blue flash would flicker and fade. The feather seemed to shimmer like a mirage. "Good. It's still fresh. Can you find his knife and my pipe?"

Near the body of the yeti, Songbird found the items. She brought them to Karl. He flipped the knife open and pricked his finger. He then smeared the blood onto the feather. It seemed to erupt in vivid intense pulses of color. He then crumpled the feather into the bowl of the pipe and said, "*Great Owl of the halfing afterlife! Guardian of pilgrim souls! Collector of both kings and paupers alike! May your silent wings pass over us! I beseech thee: redire ad vitam amico meo!*" The feather ignited as he then deeply inhaled from the pipe. Karl then blew the multicolored smoke into Toby's face. Instantly, Karl felt a sharp pain behind his right eye and his nose started to bleed.

Toby then gasped as his head righted itself as his neck untwisted and mended. His eyes shot open and he started to cough. Karl helped him sit up and patted him on the back to clear his lungs. Toby, after a few seconds, was breathing better and put his hand up to let Karl know he was okay. Hoarsely, while rubbing the back of his neck, he said, "What the hells happened? Man, my neck feels like someone twisted my head off."

Karl smiled big and said, "Well, I've got some good news and some bad news. Good news is: we had a phoenix plume. Bad news is: we needed to use a phoenix plume. The bruising should clear up normally. Otherwise, you'll be fine."

"You had one of those?" Toby asked rubbing his eyes with his right hand and propping himself up on the cold ground with the other.

"Yeah. Traded my *Doctor Monstositus's Parlour of Terror* issue number three." Karl gathered his belongings up and put them all back into his bag. "First appearance of *Streetknight the Masked Paladin* done by Zack Derby and Dan Bee."

"Oh, man, I remember when you found that book. You *loved* that book. It was the prize of your collection." Toby looked pained.

"I wouldn't say *the* prize. There are things I value more." Karl punched his friend lightly.

After a beat, Toby smiled, raised his hand up, and said, "Shaddup and help me get out of the snow, dork."

"Sir," Songbird chimed in, "You have suffered a traumatic event. Should I contact PhaedraCorp to request medical assistance?"

"No. I'll be okay. I've been mostly dead before. Good thing you guys acted so quickly. I could use a hit of miasma elixir though." Toby shook his inhaler and took two puffs. He then took a few long deep breaths and said, "*Much* better."

"I have a translation if you are ready?" She informed him.

Karl helped Toby up. Toby brushed the snow off of himself and answered, "Sure. But, no, wait." Then he asked his friend, "Karl, how did you take *that* thing down?"

Karl patted *Bartleby's Bottomless Bag*. "You can safely put living things in the bag. It takes only a few seconds to put the creature in a kind of magical stasis. This in itself isn't harmful at all. Remove the creature later and it will be as if no time had passed for it. But, when you have a portion of the living thing only partially inside the bag, it can send whatever is stuck on the threshold into shock. If it's a major organ like the brain, it can cause death." Explained Karl. "Also, the bag is capable of taking in objects of larger size than its external dimensions. But, I was just acting in the moment. I'm not sure I was really planning anything. It's all kind of hazy. The only clear thing I can recall was how angry I got."

"*Huh*. Well how come you don't get hurt when you rummage through it? I mean your hands are in it and the rest of you isn't." Asked Toby.

"Some things are a mystery." Karl shrugged, "I guess it can't hurt me because I am its owner. Maybe it just sort of senses my intent. The same way your knife just sort of knows when to pop the fire blade." Karl picked up his pipe and started to clean it out.

"Huh. Okay! Back on task." Toby returned his attention back to the matter of the sigils on the doorway. "So, Songbird, what does it all mean?"

"Simply put, it is a warning. This temple complex is as much a prison as it is a tomb. Some sort of primordial evil was entrapped within. What a society that engaged in the sacrifice of sentient beings would consider so evil as to be locked away, presumably for all time, is a matter for further study. Please understand that this translation has an *eighteen percent* chance of being in error. Regardless, I would advise caution upon entering the complex."

"Wow, you got all of that from an inscription?" Karl asked.

"I have access to vast amounts of information. I drew from many resources to not only translate the script, but also to reconstruct missing parts of the text, and hypothesize as to the societal context of the structure." She *seemed* to speak with a hint of pride.

"*Hoot*! Well, color me impressed. Let's gear up and get in there. It's time to shit or get off the pot." Declared Toby with a clap of his hands.

***

After setting up a base camp, disposing of the yeti over a cliff side, and having a meal, they inventoried their equipment and geared up in preparation for entering the temple complex. Karl had actually lost a few pounds over the past week and was pleasantly surprised to see how well the black camouflaged battle fatigues, which he had changed into before being dropped off with the supplies, fit him. He almost felt downright heroic. The PhaedraCorp logos bothered him a bit, as he didn't really see himself as the corporate employee type. He was happy when Toby pointed out that they were attached by Velcro and could be removed with ease. Toby didn't care one way or the other and kept them on.

Upon setting foot in the ruins, there was a sensation that felt like an icy finger tracing up their spines. Songbird provided light as the designated torch bearer. Her artificial skin glowed with a neon blue light that illuminated the chamber in all directions.

"Uh, Toby?" Karl's voice echoed throughout the chamber, somehow amplifying the tone of anxiety in his voice.

"Yeah." Toby responded.

"D-do you think it's possible that this place is cursed?" Karl heard the bothersome little stutter that would sometimes surface in his speech when startled or under stress. At that moment he felt the sense heroism that had existed outside simply fall away. The stutter had always made him feel a little self-conscious. It is why he spoke so rarely around people he didn't know or people he didn't like. He felt it made him sound as if he were incompetent or foolish. His former coworkers would frequently hear his stutter and see it as an opportunity for laughs at his expense.

"Oh, definitely." Said Toby, with a tinge of excitement.

"Okay. Great." Said a very unsettled Karl. He hugged his bag tightly as if it were some kind of security blanket. He quickly came to the conclusion that this wasn't, unfortunately, the proper time for the smoke he didn't get to have because of the yeti attack.

"Do you still have my knife?" asked Toby. He seemed very slightly annoyed for reasons Karl assumed had to do with being in the ruins.

"Yeah." Karl immediately removed it from his pocket and handed it over to Toby.

"Thanks." Toby gripped it tightly in his fist.

Eventually, after moving past a gauntlet of increasingly disturbing imagery carved in relief on the walls, while navigating a network of narrow, labyrinthine passages, they came to a cavernous void. Strung across it was a narrow, rickety rope bridge. Beneath it was endless shadow.

Karl felt the temple tremble. Dust and small pebbles shaken loose from the cavern ceiling rained down. He stopped in his tracks and asked aloud, "What was *that*?"

"What was what?" replied Toby.

The ground shook again. This time with enough force to knock Karl off his step. "*That*! Is this place structurally sound?"

Songbird answered, "This structure is estimated to be nearly seven thousand years old. The Ancients possessed incredibly advanced engineering and stone masonry skills. While it is understood that, over millennia without upkeep, it will has shown signs of degradation; the complex appears to be remarkably stable. Are you experiencing vertigo? Do you require more elixir to counter the thin air at this altitude, sir?"

Before Karl could answer, Toby said, "C'mon! No time to waste. Let's get across this bridge." He seemed increasingly on edge. Karl wondered if this place was affecting his friend's emotional state somehow. "Karl and I will go together. Songbird, you go last."

Toby removed a large bundle of super-strong polymer rope from his pack and then produced an auto-piton from one of his crossed double bandoliers. He slammed the metal, self-fastening, piton onto the stone ground with a loud clang, it rapidly corkscrewed itself into the ground producing a high pitched whine. Quickly, in milliseconds, it buried itself hallway into the masonry. Toby then tied the rope around himself and Karl, with enough lead behind them to cross the bridge. He anchored the rope on the piton and instructed Songbird to slowly let out more slack as the two crossed the bridge.

Toby went first. Karl could hear the bridge let out a kind of moan as his halfling friend put his weight on the bridge. A knot started to twist inside Karl's stomach. Karl hated heights.

The rope bridge began to sway gently as the two tethered friends made their way across. Karl's stomach started to rise up to his throat and he closed his eyes in the vain hope that if he couldn't see the gaping maw of the abyss beneath him that he wouldn't feel like throwing up and fainting. Karl couldn't push out of his mind the idea of how decrepit and fraying the ropes were. Not to mention how rotten and moldy the wooden planks under his feet were. The timeworn wood sagged and bowed under each step.

You don't belong here. Karl heard his step-father's voice. *What can someone like you hope to do but get in the way of others?* Cold sweat started to form on Karl's brow. He felt the blood drain away from his head. *You were always a disappointment, Karl. From the day I met you I knew you'd just be a weight around my neck.* Karl felt the tether start to pull against him as Toby edged further forward on the rickety bridge. He struggled to stave off hyperventilation and opened his eyes to inch forward. His mouth was dry and tasted acidic. *Karl, you will fall to your death. You just don't have what it takes to make it across this bridge. You are a weakling and a coward. Turn around now.*

Toby attempted to keep his focus on the far side of this cavern. He knew that he had to keep a disciplined mind to overcome the fear. Sudden movements on the edge of his vision kept distracting him. It was something above him in the darkness. He became aware of a gauze-like cloud of webbing that seemed to undulate just out of sight. He kept feeling the urge to look up. He heard soft, yet sinister, voices from no particular direction. Multiple sources of chittering murmurs that formed into disconcerting incomprehensible whispers. Try as he might to ignore it, he found himself struggling to make out what was being said, but it seemed too far off to be understood. The bridge creaked and shuddered with every step. It swayed like a pendulum as the two made their way across it.

Toby started to feel a dreadful thought invading the forefront of his mind. *Your parents. They suffer. The dangers you hurl yourself at without a though as to who will care for them; if you die, they will be defenseless against those who brutally predate upon the innocent. You've seen war. You know the harsh truth of this universe. Turn back. These people here don't understand. They couldn't possibly care about the hardships your parents must face. Your mother's heart cannot take any more strain from worry over your safety. Your father will waste away once she's gone. You can renounce this life of folly and return to the safety and security of home and hearth.*

"Karl!" Toby's voice was laden with a palpable fatigue. "Do you see something above us?!" He kept inching forward in defiance of the heartfelt desire to turn around.

"N-No! I-I can't look... I will fall!" Karl managed to barely speak. His eyes wide with fear and locked on the bottomless void below. The darkness below seemed to rise as if it was alive and meant to swallow him whole and drown him in his fears.

"Karl, I think there's something above us. I need you to scope it out. Do you see some kind of webbing?"

Karl started to feel a dull ache behind his right eye. "Toby. I don't know if I can." He said weakly. He felt his body teeter on the edge of unconsciousness.

"You've got to man! I'm trying to keep us moving forward. I need you to do this for me, Karl."

Karl swallowed down a dry lump of anxiety and slowly peeled his eyes from the terror below. For what seemed an eternity he struggled to shift his attention to the cavern ceiling. He gritted his teeth beneath lips pressed tightly together in a grimace of terror. Breathing through his nose with hurried and uneven gulps of air, Karl looked up.

He saw nothing. "Songbird! Do you see anything above us?!" Shouted Karl as he searched the ceiling for anything unusual.

"My multi-spectrum visual analysis yields no results, sir!" She replied after scanning the cavern for a second or two.

"Say what?!" Exclaimed an incredulous Toby.

"I don't see anything either, Toby." Said a confused Karl, for whom confusion began to give way to an inkling of relief and astonishment.

After a few seconds of gears slowly tumbling into place, Toby shouted, "Fuck a duck!" Toby angrily realized that this place, or the demon within it, was toying with them. "It's a hallucination!

"It's able to read us, to figure out how to manipulate us. It must also possess some ability enter our subconscious minds. To slip deeper and deeper into our psyche through our innermost insecurities." Toby extrapolated.

Once the hallucinatory attack was dismissed, the two reached the other side. Songbird reclaimed the auto-piton and Toby installed another to the ground on their side. He anchored the rope and both men reigned in the slack on the tether secured around Songbird's waist as she came across the bridge. She moved with remarkable nimbleness and shot across the bridge at an incredible pace.

After taking a break to rest and recover breath and rehydrate, the trio continued deeper into the complex. Down winding stone stairs and though echoing chambers, all decorated with detailed bas relief carvings depicting ever descending levels of the Ancient's underworld.

Karl's head had been hurting since the rope bridge. A dull thudding ache from behind his right eye. He wanted to stop and rest for a while, maybe stop and set up a small camp.

When he thought he could no longer keep up, he said, "Hey, Toby, do you think we can take a long break here? I am feeling pretty out of it right now."

Karl's vision was starting to blur from the pain, and he staggered a little and fell back. He saw Toby stop and come back to him with an inconvenienced look on his face. When Toby reached Karl he said, "Karl, why did I even bring you?"

"What? I'm sorry. I don't mean to be a bother, b-but I can barely stand, much less keep walking."

"I am sick to death of your whining." The look on Toby's face went from mild annoyance to smoldering anger.

"Toby? W-What? I-I d-don't…"

"Oh, we *all* are. My parents especially. And don't confuse their charity for genuine affection; it's pity. Because you are such a fucking loser. They think you are going to kill yourself and they are just too nice to say '*Go ahead.*' Why don't you just eat a bullet and take us out of your misery? All you do is bring everybody down." Toby's eye started to twitch and his face contorted into a disdainful sneer. He stepped forward menacingly.

"Toby!? Are you okay?" Karl edged back confused and startled.

He felt Toby shove him sharply in the shoulder and he stumbled backwards. With a hate-filled growl, Toby added, "Your step-dad was right, you know? You are too much of a pusillanimous twat to do *anything* right. And about your *mom*? Personally, I am glad she died before seeing what a fucking piece of shit you turned out to be. Although I am sure she suspected all along."

Before Karl's completely blindsided brain could respond to that vicious barb, Toby was on top of him. Karl struggled, but was too weak to fight back. Toby pinned his arms down and Karl began to cry aloud. Between hoarse screams for help, he begged Toby to stop. Karl was terrified for his life.

"KARL! SNAP OUT OF IT! *KARL*!!" Toby was on top of Karl with one of his dozen holy symbols pressed against Karl's forehead. The emerald and sapphire encrusted silver fir tree pendant known as the *Sacred Token of Hearthkeep*; the talisman of the halfling spirit of autumn and winter. Toby recited the hymn, *He Who Casts out Sorrow during the Long Night*.

The halfling saint of autumn and winter is honored during the fall feasts and winter festivals. Jolly Hearthkeep was a brawler in his youth. Large, for a halfling; and strong. In early depictions and stories, his deep red hair and fierce blue eyes conveyed perfectly the singular brashness of the young man who would rise to sainthood. As much as Jolly loved a good fight, he loved a good feast just with equal enthusiasm, if not more. The harvest meads and ciders were especially favored. As portrayed in more contemporary folklore, the deep snowy white hair of the considerably more seasoned demigod matches the intensity of his sparkling blue eyes. His girth may have expanded over the years, but his strength never waned. He is the kindly shepherd who guides his charges through the myriad changes in life and provides sanctuary and warmth in the dead of winter. In defense of his charges he will smite those who threaten their safety with a cheerful ferocity and endless endurance.

Saint Jolly Hearthkeep is also the guardian and keeper of those afflicted with melancholia and suffering from grief. For it is in the dark of winter that most seem to suffer from the absence of sunlight and the green of springtime. His symbol is a deep green fir tree with a bright blue star at its top.

Karl stopped. His swollen red eyes darted around in bewildered mortification. He was hyperventilating through his mouth because his nose was completely blocked from the pitiful wailing sobbing.

"Hey, buddy, it's *okay*. We can rest." Toby smiled. His silly grin poorly disguised his concern and relief.

"That spell you cast earlier? It must have *really* taken it out of you." Toby stood and helped his friend up. "We should've rested again before coming in here, but I was so impatient. It's a serious flaw. I'm sorry, man.

"I shrugged off the second wave, but for about four seconds I *honestly* thought you were going to steal my penknife, or even kill me for it. It has been detecting danger since we got here, but this whole place is dangerous. A little psychic nudge in the wrong direction was all it took to make me paranoid. But I could see that you were no condition to take it. There's no way in hells you would've been able to resist that psychic onslaught in your weakened state. The thin air doesn't help, either."

Karl removed a handkerchief from one of his many pockets and blew his nose. After taking a puff of elixir, Karl said, "Y-You said s-some *horrible* things." His eyes were locked on his own boots, unable to look his friend in the eye.

"Wasn't me. I am sorry you had to go through that. These demon mother fuckers are virtuosos at manipulation and subterfuge. Like I said before, if you've got a soft spot, they'll take a run at it." Toby took off his fir tree talisman and gave it to Karl. "Here, this will help. Take it. Please."

"O-Oh, N-no, I c-can't." But, Karl was too enervated to resist. Toby pinned the talisman to Karl's fatigues like a medal.

"Let's get some grub, get some rest, and put this behind us, man. I'm guessing that when a psychic blast comes in this strong, we've got to be really close to the entity's focal point or anchoring location."

"So we're almost there?" Karl asked while examining the talisman his friend gave him. He knew the autumn and winter halfling feast days were Toby's favorite times of the year.

"Exactly." Toby said. "Also, I am guessing that it probably blew its wad coming at us that hard. It's going to take some time to regroup and come at us again from a different angle. So resting now would be perfect."

Songbird was sitting nearby cross-legged with hands laid neatly in her lap in a lotus-like position.

"Songbird, you didn't see or hear anything unusual during the attacks?" inquired Toby.

"Negative, sir. No unusual readings." She said with an inexhaustibly genial voice.

Karl was drifting off when something occurred to him. "Songbird, why didn't you try to stop us from freaking out? We could've hurt each other."

"Because, Mr. Snotwaller, that would constitute a breach of my programming." She replied acquiescently.

"Huh. Can't risk harming sentient beings, or something like that?" inquired Toby.

"Something like that, yes, sir." She answered.

Karl quietly chuckled as he slipped into dreamland. "Heh. *'Blew its wad coming at us so hard.'*"

***

Songbird rose from her seated position next to the two adventurers. Karl had passed out from exhaustion and Toby was not too far off, cooking up a meal from the battlefield ration kits brought along from the base camp. She was closest to Karl. "Mr. Snotwaller, sir, I am detecting someone in distress." Songbird was kneeling beside Karl. Her mechanical hand gently nudging him back into consciousness.

Karl's grasp on the world around him consisted of the lingering headache that pounded with a dull demoralizing rhythm behind the right side of his face and being prodded awake by a blurry, glowing, mechanical lady at the end of a dark tunnel. She seemed emphatic about something. Her words were a muffled torrent of information that receded into white noise with every undulating wave of pain. He attempted to inquire as to the nature of her emergency, but what came out was a series of profanities strung together by marble-mouthed gibberish. He then fell promptly back to sleep.

Karl's dream was troubling. Lately, most of Karl's dreams had been unremarkable. It was as if the blandness of his previous hum-drum existence had seeped so deeply into his subconscious that it was infecting his dreams with banality. Upon waking, they were lost in the *Aether of Lethe*, as Karl called it. As a child, Karl had amazing Technicolor adventures into the surreal landscape made of the desperate longings and fervent hopes of a lonely little boy. Every step deeper into those bygone dreams took his dream-self deeper into a terra incognita of wonder. Every once in a while (and Karl never shared this with anyone but his mother) Karl dreamed of things that would come to pass. But, that hadn't happened in a long, long time. Not until the reoccurring dream about the stingrays on New Mars.

This new dream was one of *those* dreams. In this dream there was a girl. Her hair was like spun copper reflecting the light of a fire. Her skin was like a bowl of peaches and cream. Her eyes were bright hazel that shone like the northern lights. It seemed he knew her, intimately, but he couldn't recall her name somehow. He was back on Sojourn with her. They were holding hands watching stars being born in a rainbow colored nebula that pulsed with every new sun coming alive.

Behind them something crept. Unseen by the lovers lost in the rapture of the sublime sights before them, it stalked closer. A many-legged monstrosity cloaked somehow in darkness. Obscured by what seemed to be the very stuff of night, Karl, as the dreamer, couldn't make it out. But as it moved in closer to his dream-self and the petite beauty beside him, he could hear its insect-like claws each tapping on the ground with each advance. His dream-self started to become aware of the threat, as he began to notice strange murmuring whispers underneath the sounds of Sojourn swimming through the void of space. The regal beauty beside him was oblivious to the danger. She simply smiled and looked at him with a warmth that radiated from her lovely face that shone directly into his heart.

Then a long, black, gnarled, spikey claw impaled her through the chest from behind and the light went out in her eyes as blood and tiny chucks of viscera splattered all over Karl's face.

Karl awoke with a yelp and sat straight up.

Songbird was seated about two yards away in a lotus position. Toby was not too far off performing a minor culinary miracle with

PhaedraCorp standard issue field rations. Karl's head felt fuzzy and his right eye felt like he had been punched very hard.

Songbird turned to him and said, "Mr. Snotwaller, sir, I was about to wake you. I am detecting someone in distress"

The strange electric tingles of deja vu ran down Karl's spine. He suspected that he was dreaming. Karl looked all round him; things seemed real. He rubbed his face with both hands and then ran them through his hair as if to sweep the lingering sleep from his body.

Upon coming to the conclusion that this was reality, he asked, "What do you hear? I don't hear anything."

"My hearing is several times more sensitive than yours and can detect noises in a much larger range of frequency. I can detect electromagnetic frequencies outside of the normal range of human ability. I am picking up what I believe to be a distant cry for help. Female. Young. High stress levels. Most likely Sarah Phaedra."

Karl asked, "Where is she?" as he got up and started to bundle up his gear.

"It has stopped, but I believe I can make an estimation of which direction to head. I will continue to analyze my internal recordings to discern her general direction. This may take some time as it was so distant as to be on the very edge of my ability to perceive." Songbird sat still and her neon blue aura flickered slightly.

"Good morning, princess, sleep well?" Toby handed Karl a plastic spork and a warm paper cup filled with a steaming stew-like concoction. "Chow time. Dude, you've *got* to try this." Toby breathed in the aroma and let it dance on his pallet for a moment before grabbing a spork and digging in like a rabid badger eating waffles at a truck stop after a night of intense drinking and bad decisions.

With a mouthful of stew Toby asked, "So, what's with her?"

"She thinks she can hear the girl. She's trying to figure out if she can tell where the sound is coming from." Karl started to eat. The stew was surprisingly savory, even though Karl's normally sharp taste buds couldn't quite determine what sort of (or if any) meat was being used.

Best not to think on it for too long, thought Karl and he continued eating.

Songbird came out of her trance about the time they were done packing up the temporary camp in preparation to continue exploring deeper into the temple complex. "My acoustic study is complete. I am reasonably certain that I can lead you towards the area from where she cried out."

"After you." Said Toby as he slung his pack onto his back. Karl grabbed his bag and together they followed Songbird deeper into the ruins.

***

As they ventured deeper into the heart of the ruined temple complex, the air became difficult to breath. It was as if it had become fouled with the increasing sense of oppression and evil that saturated this place. Toby and Karl had to slap on atmospheric filter masks to continue. Fortunately, these models (the *TrekTech II*) had a slot attachment where one could insert a standard issue micro-canister of the miasma elixir and an easy to read meter so that the wearer knows when the filter and micro-canister needed to be replaced. It was remotely connected to a wrist monitor and would automatically release a dose to the wearer as needed. *PhaedraCorp Expeditionary R&D really thought of everything*, thought Karl.

While Songbird could see in total darkness, she gave off a soft blue glow to illuminate the ruins for Toby. It was becoming increasingly less effective due to some mysterious supernatural effect in this place. Karl's goblin heritage meant that he had pretty remarkable night vision and suffered much less from the lack of proper lighting. The shadows, as the three went deeper, seemed as if they would not be dismissed so easily by their glowing automaton companion. The shadows seemed to greedily smother the light. Toby had to ready his special goggles, they allowed the wearer to see farther in low light conditions. It could also extrapolates the location of ghosts, within twenty feet, if they were present, by detecting minute amounts of a kind of radiation given off by ectoplasmic residue as it begins to breaks down. However, using them for extended periods of time could cause serious eye fatigue and repeated use could permanently impair normal vision. Toby preferred to let them rest just above his eyes, on his forehead, kept in place by their leather straps which buckled behind his head. When they were not in use, he made due by using the penknife's flaming blade as a torch.

Toby felt that they were on the right track when they came to an area where the tunnels were coated in thick lairs of webbing. Toby's weapon easily burned through the webs. Gauze-like wall after wall of sticky silky material choked the passages. It all recoiled and curled away into blackened withered ash and flew off into the currents of wind that circulated the fetid air in these forgotten tunnels. It was almost as if the webbing itself was a large nervous system sending shudders throughout its whole body as parts were burnt away. Karl couldn't help but feel an increasing sense of danger as he progressed into the webs.

Songbird lead them to a large chamber covered in bleached bone white blankets of webs. Songbird's blue aura reflected of it like moonlight from sea foam as the webbing here seemed to dance with blue firelight. There was a large stone sarcophagus, slightly ajar, in the center of the chamber. Trapped, pinned against the far wall by a coat of webbing, was a girl in some kind of space suit.

Karl could not see her face, but there was something familiar about her. He pushed past Songbird and Toby to see if she was alive. Around her neck, tethered by a thin leather strap, was a fist-sized blood-red gemstone that reflected no light, but instead swirled and rippled menacingly from deep within.

Karl was only a few steps away from her when they all heard something large drop from the ceiling behind them. A guttural hissing voice filled with clicks, as if agonizingly forced from a throat not built for humanoid speech said, "*Mine!*"

"Holy fuck nuggets!" yelled Toby upon turning to see what just made its entrance into the sarcophagus chamber.

What he saw was some sort of unholy union of arachnid and humanoid. It was adroitly perched atop the monolithic stone coffin, belying its hulking size. It was crouching above them, but it must have stood at least eight feet tall on bipedal digigrade legs. It was pure white except for its coal black eyes and a blood red hourglass pattern on its bulbous spider abdomen. Fine spiny hairs covered its pure white chitinous skin. Adjoined above the abdomen was a humanoid torso with two huge arms at its broad powerful shoulders. Underneath, (on its "belly") twitched four quick tiny arms. Each arm, and both feet, ended in three, long, razor-sharp claws. Its head and facial features resembled a fanged humanoid skull with an oversized pair of deep set eyes. Eyes that were fixed on Karl. Six tiny, black, beady eyes on its brow swiveled to take in its surroundings in an unblinking sweep of the chamber. Instead of a lower jaw, it had two massive spider-like mandibles ending in dagger-like fangs. From those fangs venom dripped and oozed.

"No! Pretty *mine*!" It scraped the words out of its abomination mouth and charged at Karl. It rushed halfway across the chamber and slapped him away from the girl.

Karl felt as if he had been hit with a sledge hammer as he was knocked across the room. The filter mask flew off of his face and bounced into a corner. He hit the ground hard and he felt a sharp pain in his lower back. Karl gasped like a fish out of water as he reached out to recover his filter mask from where he thought it landed. He sifted through dusty webbing to find his mask before he passed out. The blow he took set off a throbbing klaxon of pain on the right side of his face.

As he desperately searched for his mask, he could hear Toby engage the freakish monstrosity with a frenzied battle cry. A split-second later the spider-thing let out a loud hiss of pain. He was grateful that Toby was engaging the horror and drawing it away from him. Each slash was joined with the sound of this Nightmare Queen's alien flesh being seared away. The odor of burning meat and hair filled Karl's nose.

When Karl finally found his mask and quickly clapped it over his face, his lips were just beginning to turn blue. Through bleary, water filled eyes he saw Toby dance around this monster, his flaming sword flaying chunks of chitin off of it. Its thick white blood sizzled and danced off of the sword's fiery edge. Karl tried to get up and get to the girl while Toby was distracting the monster, and that's when he felt something very wrong with his back.

There was a blazing hot flash of pain in his lower back. It was as if someone had taken a rusty bone saw that had been hooked to a car battery and was slowly grinding it across his spine. His legs wouldn't move. They simply twitched feebly as he convulsed with pain. The blow had aggravated his old injury.

***

When Karl was twelve years old, he decided that he needed a way to deal with all the bad things that had happened to him in his life. He was keenly aware that he carried around much anger and shame inside. The alienation and poverty, the callous dismissals and the cruel rejections; it was all much more than a lonesome boy could bear. Karl lived in dread of the day when his rage would break its chains and unleash a lifetime of pain on some unsuspecting bully; or worse, someone he loved. For Karl, it was far worse to become like the animals that hurt him, than to suffer in silence the abuse that the world heaped upon him.

More than once he had returned home bloodied and bruised when he couldn't run fast enough or hide well enough. He would lie to his mother and tell her that it was just another accident. His mother worried, because there seemed to be too many accidents for just one small boy.

There came a day when Karl couldn't run anymore; when he had become sick of hiding. He wanted to fight back. But, he also wanted to be in control of that impulse. Out ahead of it somehow, steering it away from the people he cared about. Karl suspected that something monstrous was deep inside him. Ugliness and poison put there by people who hurt him. He refused to let that murderous rage boiling up inside him dictate who he was.

Karl set himself on a quest. He was going to learn the secrets of self-discipline and self-defense. He was going to learn the martial arts. He searched through libraries reading about styles, and wandered through the town inquiring about schools. No one wanted to teach a goblin half-breed, much less one who couldn't pay. But Karl never gave up. Every day after school and until his mother came home from her two jobs, he dedicated his time to finding a teacher. Instead of homework, he would read books about various martial philosophies, the history and development of weapons, and he would pour over the scant scraps of information regarding the legendary secret powers of martial artists. This was his life for nearly two years.

Then, one day, Karl found a teacher who didn't say no. A stern, laconic dark elf who agreed to train Karl in basic self-defense techniques in exchange for his service after school. Karl was to clean up the training hall, wash uniforms, mop bathrooms, and whatever errands the master needed done. In exchange, so long as it didn't interfere with his other pupils' learning, he would have some of his students teach Karl rudimentary skills.

Karl was ecstatic. He saw every time he was used as a punching dummy as an opportunity for learning. Every moment sweeping, or washing around the hall gave him a chance to watch the others practice. He would diligently repeat what he had seen when he got home. His mother noticed that he was away much more and seemed happier, and hungrier. She assumed he had made new friends. She was happy that Karl was finally starting to settle in to a childhood.

The other students tormented Karl. They pushed him as far as they thought they could get away with. Their master did not tolerate such "lack of focus" and would discipline them if he caught them bullying him. So they quickly learned to mask the punishment they enjoyed pouring out on Karl as "training." Karl took it all in stride. He would relive each attack in his mind to analyze their tactics and learn from his mistakes. Eventually, Karl would welcome the confrontations just to practice theory. His refusal to back down is what attracted the attention of the master's daughter, Artemis.

Moved by sympathy for his plight, she decided to train him, *really* train him, on her own. In secret, she would sneak away to visit him at his home on the weekends. Karl eagerly soaked up all she could show him. He became obsessed with driving himself to be better. He wanted to earn the respect of his fellow students and his master. Over time, her pity became respect. Her respect became friendship. And when that friendship blossomed into something unexpected, they knew that it was forbidden by her father and that it would bring the ridicule of society at large, but they surrendered to it.

The master had a very strict rule that his daughter was to be treated with the utmost respect. No student would ever be allowed to court her. Her father frequently reminded her that any sort of fraternization with his students was expressly forbidden. Especially the *"goblin boy."*

In a matter of mere months he had surpassed everyone else in the class, except the master and his daughter. Karl had fallen in love with his master's daughter. It was his first love. Karl let his young, naïve, heart take the reins and blinded himself to any other possibility than being in love forever.

Eventually, secrets get out. Some of the students got together and decided to spy on Karl. They wanted to see how he had gotten so good so quickly. The very next evening, the master called a special class together. He brought Karl front and center and confronted him about the transgression.

Made to feel ashamed and unable to look up from the ground; terrified and thinking only to spare her the same shame in having to confess that she had loved him, Karl emphatically denied any feelings for Artemis in front of the entire class. His heart broke when he looked up from his shoes to see the wounded look on her face. With tears streaming down out of her once proud and carefree eyes, she slapped him and ran out of the hall. The master then banished Karl and informed him that starting in one hour, should he decide to show up there, at the training hall, or *anywhere* near his daughter again, that he would declare amnesty to any and all who would beat him to death on the spot. He then closed into Karl's face, looked him dead in the eyes and softly said *"Run half-breed."* Stunned by what just transpired, he wandered aimlessly from the training hall in a daze and hid nearby until the master dismissed the class. Karl then watched, hidden in the shadows, as Artemis and her father drove off in the rain. But he felt that he couldn't go home. He couldn't leave things like this. He had given into fear and made a horrible mistake. He wanted to make things right. He imagined and hoped that he could fix what had been broken.

Karl ran to their house, through the cold wet night, to beg forgiveness from Artemis and her father. In his naivety and desperation, he could not have anticipated that this event would escalate quickly and unexpectedly into a seminal moment in his life. The master was incensed. He felt that his home was trespassed upon and his daughter violated. The enraged dark elf attacked Karl with a ferocity that he had never encountered before. How does one explain themselves to someone who is so taken over by anger that they simply will not reason? Karl defended himself for as long as he could. He focused all of his meager skills on narrowly defending himself from wave after wave of attack. In a moment of weakness and frustration, compounded by his incensed state, the master used an obscure maneuver and shattered Karl's defenses; the master broke Karl's back. Passing out from the pain in the mud and rain, the last thing he heard was his former master, through tears of rage and perhaps even guilt, swearing that he regretted the day Karl darkened his doorstep.

The very next day, as Karl laid in a hospital, Artemis and her father packed up and moved far away. Karl never heard from her again.

He was devastated. That was the year that he learned a valuable lesson about love, trust, and how people would look at him for the rest of his life. He would always be seen as something that just doesn't fit; as a *half-breed*. With only his mother to nurse him back to health, it took two years of rehabilitation before he could walk close to normally again.

He learned to focus past the pain. To swallow it down and carry on. He never shared the truth about how he was hurt with his mother. It would only upset her. Karl made up a story about a bad fall while attempting to rescue a cat stuck in a tree at night during a storm. He wasn't sure if she bought it, but she seemed to understand that he wasn't ready to deal with the truth yet.

To this day, Karl has a slight limp and constant pain radiating from his back, down his left leg.

***

"Karl... Karl, you okay?!" shouted Toby as he continued to lure the monster away from his friend.

"I think it broke my back!" Karl shouted at Toby.

Karl experienced an inexplicably profound urgency to help the girl trapped in the webs and resolved himself to that task. He relied upon the mantra that had served him throughout his life when he needed to push through pain. *Pain is in the mind. The mind can be controlled. There is no pain.* Karl took a deep breath and steadied himself for the agony that lay ahead.

After catching his breath and doing his best to keep only the mantra in the forefront of his mind, he dragged himself to the girl. With each advance towards her a new wave of pain hit him. It would slam into him with nerve shattering intensity just as the last wave was fading into a background ocean of bone-deep ache.

Pain is in the mind. The mind can be controlled. There is no pain. Again and again in his mind, the words were like a dam against the steady flow of suffering.

Though her all-environment survival suit had no markings, it was clearly of PhaedraCorp design. It was so well designed that, from where he was, he could see that her filter was red-lining and the canister slot was empty. Karl had replacement filters and spare canisters of elixir. The design was incredibly user friendly. Simply eject old filter and slap a new on in, then slip a canister into the slot designed for it. Karl just had to *stand up*.

Songbird had managed to slip past the arachnid monster while it was completely distracted with the fight. She began to try to remove the girl from the webbing.

Toby was starting to show signs of exhaustion. He had been using his size and agility to great advantage while nickel and diming his opponent. Toby methodically, doggedly, was chipping away at the horror's defenses.

"I-Is she okay?" Karl grunted as he gritted his teeth through the pain and shakily attempted to rise.

"Her vital signs are weak, but steady. She has been trapped here for several days relying on the survival suit to keep her alive." Songbird continued to free her from the gluey restraints.

Karl's trembling legs gave out and he fell at Songbird's feet. He landed with a grunt and after a few moments, he began again to try and get up onto his feet.

"Mr. Snotwaller, please remain still. You are severely injured." Songbird suggested with an eerie calm.

"I have more filters. Get her down to me." instructed Karl.

Songbird tore at the clinging fibers binding the young woman. Once she had been freed, Songbird laid the girl down gently near Karl. He quickly replaced the filter and installed a canister into her helmet. With a simple ding, the suit acknowledged the insertion of the new filter and began to pump fresh air and elixir into her suit.

She started to breathe easier and deeper. In a matter of seconds, her eyes opened. She woke with a start and her eyes struggled to take in her surroundings. Hoarsely she said, "*The gem*. Put it in the sarco-sarcophagus." With great effort, she tore lose the gemstone around her neck and with some difficulty managed to slide it towards Karl. She then faded back into unconsciousness.

Before Karl could reach the demon stone, Toby delivered a toppling blow to the arachnid monster. The spider-thing collapsed and an exhausted, yet victorious, Toby staggered around its corpse to decapitate the fiendish abomination. Barely able to lift his blazing sword to deliver the coup de grace, he was breathing heavily. With his back to Karl and Songbird, he was poised to dispatch the Nightmare Queen.

But before he could deliver the final blow, Songbird swiftly stepped up to him saying, "Mr. Seven Hills, I apologize that this has become necessary." Songbird reached out and touched Toby and what looked like a blast of bright blue lightning flickered from her fingers with a deafening crack. It passed through Toby and scortched the webbing and stone on the wall beyind him. Toby seized up and crumpled into a smoking heap. His knife extinguished and fell beside him.

"Toby!" Karl cried out for his friend.

"Mr. Snotwaller, I cannot allow you to put this demon back in its sarcophagus prison." She stepped over Karl and swiftly snatched the gemstone from out of his reach. "I can see that the integrity of its gemstone containment spell is dangerously wavering and I will require your body to host this spirit until so that I may return to Mr. Phaedra both his stolen demon and his prodigal daughter. Your incapacitated physical condition will make it far easier to overpower and load you into the cryogenic stasis pod Mr. Phaedra sent along with your supplies. You have my deepest apologies, Mr. Snotwaller, as you will not survive the process of extraction. Mr. Seven Hill's indomitable mental fortitude would've made him ill-suited for that purpose, so he was eliminated."

"No." Karl's voice resonated with a quiet fury. His voice intoned the pure rage and grief of this betrayal, and of all those that came before.

"The Nightmare Queen is the last of her kind, it would be criminal to destroy the last of a species. When she awakes, she will finish off Mr. Seven Hills. It will appear to be another expedition gone horribly wrong. Exactly like the research team eighty years ago." Songbird gently laid her hand on Sarah Phaedra. "For what it's worth, thank you, Mr. Snotwaller. I am sincerely grateful that we reached Sarah in time. I have been her governess and constant companion since she was seven years old and would have been greatly distressed by her loss."

"No." Karl repeated angrily in fearless defiance. Something from deep within him was rushing to the surface like the surge of magma before a volcanic explosion that had been too long contained.

Songbird retrieved Toby's penknife and examined the edge. "This should suffice. Mr. Snotwaller, please do you best to remain still as I make my incision." With the red demon stone in hand she approached Karl.

"*NO!!!*" Karl roared. His eyes rolled back and a gust of wind rippled through the webs. Songbird turned around to look when she heard the huge stone door to the sarcophagus fly open.

"Mr. Snotwaller, perhaps we might negotiate..." she was cut off when some sort of invisible hand picked her up and slammed her with great force into the ceiling high above. The impact caused her to release her grip on the knife and gemstone and they fell to the ground. Then the unseen force piledrove her into the ground leaving a crater-like indentation in the stone. Her broken body rose up from that cracked depression in the cold hard ground. One arm was hanging, mangled and barely attached to her torso. "Meh- Mr. Snotwaller, you sta-a-a-a-a-a-and to pro-profit..." she said with a warbled mechanical voice.

"Fuck you."

Songbird was violently whipped into the sarcophagus by the invisible hand. The demon stone quickly rose up from the ground, seemingly of its own accord, and flew with great speed at her. With a terrible strength driving it, the nearly fist-sized jewel lodged between her broken lips. Then it was as if something mightily kicked the gemstone down her mouth, wedging it inside the opening of her throat and dislocating her lower jaw before the stone lid slammed shut with a thunderous boom. The whole object then grinded backwards, with a great and cacophonous wailing of stone on stone, into the far wall of the chamber before backing up and furiously slamming thunderously twice more into the wall leaving thick cracks in the masonry and partially embedding the sarcophagus into the rock wall. As the fading echoes of what had just happened vanished into the distant ruined hallways, a dust settled over the increasing quiescence.

Karl shuddered let out a gasp as his nose began to bleed profusely. His bloodshot eyes rolled back down just before he passed out covered in cold sweat. His last hazy thought was, *Huh. Well, I certainly never thought it would end like this*. Then nothing. Blackness.

***

Karl saw his mother. She was as if the world had been far kinder to her than it had actually been in her life. She was young again, and healthy, and happy. She looked at him warmly and smiled.

"Mom? Momma, is that *you*?"

She embraced him and stroked the hair on the back of his head just like she used to when he was little. He could smell the gentle perfume of the lotion she always used and feel her soft hair, much longer than it had been in life, drape down her back as he hugged her tightly.

"Mom, I've missed you *so* much…" Karl began to cry and she gently shushed him and wiped away his tears.

"Mom, where am I?" he asked.

"Safe. You were very brave, Karl. I am very proud of you."

"Am I *dead*?" He was starting to remember what happened in the ruins.

"There's no such thing as death, honey. Karl, I want you to remember something: *Everything will be okay*. Even if things look bad, it will work out fine. All right, sweetheart?" She beamed with pride and tenderly fixed his disheveled hair. She smiled at him again and kissed his cheek softly.

"I will, Mom."

***

Karl awoke in gradual stages, becoming progressively more aware that he wasn't alone. Once his lucidity hit a critical mass, his bleary eyes opened slowly to see the bright light of day coming through a hospital window. He could see tubes coming out of his arms and wires connecting him to a machine producing steady slow beeps. A television was running softly in the background. The sterilized smell of a hospital always put Karl on edge. It was as if the place was trying to ineffectually hide from death. He turned his head to see October seated next to him, asleep in a chair.

Karl, to say the least, was confused. He tried to speak but his throat was too hoarse to make much more than a dry, creaking whisper. That is when Bill, hunched down to fit through the doorframe, entered the room with two paper cups filled with hot beverages.

"Honey, he's awake!" exclaimed Bill.

October's eyes blinked open and she smiled. She gave Karl a quick hug and said, "Hold on!" before running out of the room and into the next room. Bill just blinked, took a sip from a ridiculously small paper cup, and waved.

Not long after, October returned with Mr. and Mrs. Seven Hills.

"Oh my goodness!" said Mrs. Seven Hills and she came to Karl's bedside to give him a hug.

"Hey there, son! How you feeling?" inquired Toby Senior as he gently patted Karl's shoulder.

"I think I'm okay. How did I get here? How did you guys get here? Where's Toby? Is he okay?"

"I'm still listed as your emergency contact." said October. "Bill and I got here as soon as we could after we got the call that you were in the hospital." She continued, "Apparently, someone named Sarah Phaedra found you both in some ruins, called for help, and saved both of you. Toby was hurt pretty badly."

"Wait... *She* saved *us*?"

"That's what the local news has been going on about for the last seventy two hours." October found the remote control. The news was on and she turned up the volume.

"...amazing story of Sarah Phaedra, the sole heiress to a vast interstellar corporate fortune who rescued two hikers in the mountains on the same day her father was indicted on no less that thirty-two capital felonies. Crimes including fraud, tax evasion, treason, conspiracy..."

Karl's jaw dropped a little. "That's not what happened."

A voice from the doorway chimed in. "It's not like anyone could actually ask the two of you. You've both been unconscious for nearly four days." Sarah said as she entered the room in a wheelchair. She was accompanied by a graceful automaton pushing her chair.

Karl, nearly jumped out of his skin at the sight of the clockwork servant, for it was nearly identical to Songbird.

"Mr. Snotwaller, you don't need to be afraid. *Echo* is harmless." Sarah reassured him.

"Can it wait outside, please?" asked a very uneasy Karl.

"Well, that's a disturbing new phobia!" October half-jokingly quipped.

Karl sighed and looked at her with tired eyes.

"*What*? I thought it was kind of funny." She said quietly and shrugged as she took a sip of herbal tea from her paper cup. Karl managed a weak smile to reassure her that ordinarily it might've been.

"Echo, please wait outside for me."

"Yes, ma'am." Echo left the room.

"Thank you." said Karl. "Now, where is Toby? The News said you rescued us both. Is he okay?"

Mr. and Mrs. Seven Hills looked at each other with troubled eyes. Toby Senior held his wife and answered, "Son, Toby hasn't woken up. The doctors say that he is out of the woods, but can't even hazard a guess as to when, or if, he will come out of the coma." Mrs. Seven Hills began to quietly cry in his arms and he did his best to comfort her.

"Sir, Ma'am, I want you both to know that no matter what happens, I owe your son and Karl my life and I will pay to have the best specialists brought in to treat him." Said Sarah. "Karl and Toby don't have to worry about the medical costs. It will all be taken care of."

Speechless, Toby Sr. took her hand and nodded his deeply felt appreciation. Mrs. Seven Hills hugged Sarah and kissed her on the cheek.

"May I see him?" asked Karl.

"You've been through a lot, Karl. Maybe…" said October.

"Look, either you help me to him, or I crawl there with my ass hanging out of this fucking gown." Karl began to pull wires and tubes out of himself as he furiously attempted to kick his tightly tucked sheets off. The machines which had been monitoring his vital signs began to let out a stream of electronic chirps and wails. Frustratedly he shouted, "Who in the hells tucked me into bed, *the Marquis DeSade*?"

"Okay, cool your engines. No one needs to see your butt flashing the whole hospital. C'mon." October helped him out of bed and with a look towards Bill she made her will known to her gigantic husband. Bill gingerly picked Karl up and made his way to the next room.

Before they got to the door, a rather dour looking half-elven nurse with fatigued eyes that belied her youth arrived to block them. "Sir! This is unacceptable! You need to get back to bed *immediately*!" she bellowed exasperatedly.

"Out of the way, or I'll have bridge troll strip your pretty floral scrubs off and toss you into the parking lot." Barked Karl. It's possible he had every intention of following through on the threat.

The nurse froze in place like a deer caught in headlights. As the pieces of this puzzle started to tumble into place in her mind, her expression changed to one of stymied resignation and she stepped aside. October couldn't help but let out a choked snort as she nearly shot tea out of her nose at the spectacle.

Echo, who stood at the ready just outside the door, began to ask if he was all right. Karl stifled her, "Quiet, you! *Scat*!" He furiously dismissed her with an irate flourish of his hand.

Toby looked as if he were peacefully sleeping. The machines he was hooked up to cheerfully chirped a slow, rhythmic, story of his stability. The electrical burns from the bolt of lightning entering his back and exiting his chest were nearly completely healed, but he would have some scars.

Bill set Karl down in a chair next to Toby's bed. Karl took his friend's hand, careful not to disconnect any wires or tubes. "Hey, buddy. We made it out. With all our parts intact. *More or less*. So, it's time to hit the Arena. You know how you're always saying that chicks dig scars."

If Toby could hear Karl, he showed no evidence of it.

An ibis-headed doctor in a white lab coat entered the room followed by the long-suffering half-elven nurse. With a slight accent the doctor said, "Mr. Snotwaller, good morning. I'm Dr. Khmun." He made some notes on a clip board he had in his hands. After a few moments of scanning charts and initialing, he clicked his pen and slid it into his front coat pocket. He then passed the clip board off to the nurse who left the room. "I have been taking care of you and your friend. Good to see you up and about." He produced a medical scanner from his coat pocket and began to examine Karl.

After a concise examination the doctor said, "I don't see why you can't be discharged today, Karl. But, take it easy for a week or so. If you feel fatigued, listen to your body and rest. Do not hesitate to return if you feel sick, okay? I am serious. Check yourself in, or come and see me if you have any concerns. In the meantime, you should be fine with over the counter medications for any discomfort or pain."

"What about Toby?" Karl asked.

"He has made an amazing recovery and shows no signs of brain damage. At this point we've done all we can do. We are doing our best to ensure his comfort and now it's simply a waiting game. I believe that it's only a matter of time before he wakes up." Dr. Khmun reassured. "In perhaps a week or so, if Toby's condition continues to remain stable, he will be transferred to a facility that specializes in long term care and can provide him with the best doctors, rehabilitation, and medical technology money can buy."

Karl couldn't help but quietly cry at his best friend's bedside. "Do you think he can hear me, doc?"

Dr. Khmun placed a reassuring hand on Karl's shoulder and said, "There's almost no way to be absolutely certain, Karl, but many people report that while in comas like Toby's they were aware of their surroundings. Personally, I believe that talking with him can only help. The *both* of you."

***

In the next few weeks, Karl sat by his friend. The nurses and doctors had come to know Karl and allowed him to stay there overnight with Toby. Sometimes he would read to Toby, usually what Karl referred to as *essential* comic book reading. Karl would describe the images and the action and make note of which character said what. Karl played several classic action movies that they had seen together many times before. Karl felt that it was better because Toby already knew what was happening on screen and could enjoy the movie despite being unable to see it. Karl attempted to play several hands of cards and even forayed into chess with limited success.

Toby was receiving his nutrients through a tube, so Karl would describe his meals to Toby in the hopes that Toby would be so jealous that he would be forced to wake up in order to eat a real meal. At first it made him feel a little bit guilty, but he justified it by deciding that it was for a good cause; to bring back his friend.

When the pretty nurse arrived for his bath time or when the physical therapists were helping maintain Toby, Karl would go for a walk. Sometimes to pick up a few comic books or grab a snack. Sometimes he would go sit under the trees outside and sneak a smoke of his pipe. He had actually obtained a prescription and took every opportunity to avail himself of it.

The Crumbling Mountains of the Elder Beasts were visible from the hospital. They looked different now to Karl. A bitter sweetness at the thought that somehow a piece of their mystery had been lost. Another new sensation also, deep inside and no less moving, for Karl had survived something incredible in those mountains. He had lived in the face of impossible odds and that seemed to have granted him an infinitesimal measure of the grandeur that those mountains possessed.

Sarah would visit every day. Initially, she agreed to leave Echo outside in the sky car. She would bring food or a game to play with Karl. Sometimes she sat in on movie nights. Karl didn't even mind her asking questions over the movies because he had seen them so many times and it was nice to have some actual conversation.

Karl began to look forward to her visits and even let her read to Toby once. For the first time in her life she was beginning to feel as if she had an actual friend. In time, Sarah managed to convince Karl to let it assist them occasionally. She had found a way to help Karl get past his experience with Songbird. It was at that moment, in the realization of what she had helped him do, that Karl truly felt something move in his heart.

It helped that Karl felt Echo was somehow, inexplicably different from Songbird. Even Sarah admitted to not feeling the connection with

Echo she had with her previous automaton. In spite of being much more advanced, it was as if Echo lacked some spark, some ethereal mysterious quality that Songbird possessed.

As their trust in each other grew, Karl learned more about what had happened from her. She explained not only her part in all of this, but also what she had uncovered in her own investigations into her father's activities. Investigations that had begun years earlier with the death of her mother, but had resulted in the uncovering of a well-hidden trail of events going back nearly two centuries.

***

Her father had always used his power, wealth, and influence to safeguard his privacy. This paranoid obsession with isolation was imperative, for should the family secret get out (about the pact with the ancient demon) he would be ruined. Icarian was an incredibly intelligent engineer, entrepreneur, and tactician, as well as an expert at playing the game of public relations. Eighty years ago, when he discovered that a scholastic investigation of the ruins was underway, he rushed to fund it. His patronage granted him access to every detail of the discovery and every aspect of the project. He spent a fortune not only equipping the team, and developing new technologies for their project, but also documenting the project for posterity. He then had the research team eliminated and destroyed all evidence of their camp. His highly publicized funding, and the subsequent loss, of the Precursor Temple Project seemingly eliminated any suspicion of his true motives and activities. Following the disappearance, he played to part of the brokenhearted patron of exploration whose inspired vision of discovery had crumbled and then he seemed to quietly withdraw into his private life. He spun for himself the identity of a courageous visionary turned tragic recluse.

Karl was confused about the chain of events in her story. The Precursor Temple Project disappearance happened *eighty years* ago, how could Icarian Phaedra IV have been involved? Karl met him, he would've been a much older man.

Sarah went on to explain that the secret he protected went beyond the demonic source of his wealth and power. The truth he hid from the outside world, what he guarded with maleficent determination from within his high security compound at the foot of the Crumbling Mountains was that *he* was the first Icarian Phaedra. A part of what he received in exchange for binding his soul to the infernal spirit he unleashed in the ruins was a form of near immortality. There was an additional price: he lost the ability to sire children and thereby establish a true dynasty. Every few decades he would fake his own death and leave all of his fortune and control of his vast corporate empire to himself, posing as his own namesake son. He fabricated documentation of birth, education, and whatever else was needed to convince the outside worlds that he was simply a descendant bearing a remarkable likeness to his father, grandfather, and then great grandfather.

Icarian had made enemies during his rise to power. Nearly twenty years ago a near miss during an assassination attempt made him realize that he needed a legitimate heir should the worst come to pass. While he did not age or succumb to illness, he could be murdered under very specific circumstances. Icarian Phaedra had learned over the century to become nothing if not the sort of man who prepared for contingencies. He recruited a surrogate mother and using cutting edge science and technology, alongside obscure and dangerous mystical rites, created synthetic DNA which he then used to create a kind of clone; a perfect daughter. Sarah was an amazing child, she was a good hearted and precocious genius who's insatiable curiosity and endless fascination to the most minute of details propelled her past her peers on a scholastic level. She would also prove to be the downfall of Icarian Phaedra.

Sarah's mother was selected from thousands of willing surrogate candidates for her excellent physical fitness, remarkable intelligence, and prolific talents. She legally married Icarian and agreed to give birth to his heirs in return for her substantial debts being erased. She raised Sarah largely by herself as a prisoner to his obsession with privacy inside his fortress-like palatial estate. While Icarian would check in from time to time to see how his progeny was coming along, Sarah's mother could see over the years that something dark lurked within Icarian. He could be cold, callous, and emotionally brutal. While she might be able to bear the brunt of his neglect and cruelty, she could not allow her daughter to suffer through it. When Sarah was seven years old she asked Icarian for a divorce. She insisted upon full custody of her beloved daughter. She demanded that they both be set free. Soon after, she vanished.

Songbird was given to Sarah when she was seven years old by her father; the winter her mother was declared dead. Her father presented this advanced prototype as a governess, tutor, and confidant before shipping the child off to boarding school. Icarian designed the automaton to be the perfect companion and protector for his daughter. A foster mother that he could carefully and precisely control. Her childhood had been, with the exception of Songbird's constant companionship, a lonesome one. Sarah discovered at an early age that people were either afraid of her father or trying to use her to get to him. Songbird was her only true friend while away from home attending the best private boarding schools.

There may have been a time after his daughter was born when Icarian thought he could forge a new better destiny. That the possibility existed of some redemption for his blood stained soul. As the years passed and he had been drawn further and further into the webs of corruption woven by the demon was bound to, he ultimately resigned himself to that evil course. He came to believe it pointless to resist. There were brief moments where might have taken pride in his daughter's achievements. He might have even longed to feel a genuine fatherly affection for his daughter, for even the most worn-thin and poisonous of souls may desperately wish for love. For Icarian had some inkling of what the girl was going through.

He himself was an orphan from the slums of the floating asteroid mining city of Anvil (in the Chain of Tears asteroid belt, in the Pyre system.) It was only by his intellect, business acumen, and ruthlessness did he rise out of that squalor. He was a middle aged owner of a used and broken-down mining freighter who was barely able to pay his crew regularly when he stumbled into greatness. Some last lingering part of him that was good could not bear the thought of his daughter suffering alone as he did growing up. Songbird was as much an attempt to comfort his grieving child as she was a way to ensure his dynastic ambitions would be protected.

Sarah graduated with honors from high school at eleven years of age and attained an undergraduate degree in just two and a half years from New Mars' most prestigious university. She completed her doctorate in Linguistics and Artificial Intelligence in another three years. She wrote the language translator software in Songbird and was recognized as a prodigy in the fields of cryptography and computing.

For most of her life, Sarah had always been keenly aware of her mother's absence even though she could barely remembered her. It was this lingering and deeply felt ache that propelled her to investigate the circumstances of her mother's death. Sarah took her first shaky steps into what would become a secret inquiry into her mother's true identity and the mysterious circumstances of her death nearly a year before attaining her doctorate degree. The precocious young girl had grown into a capable young woman who needed answers and was finally able to pursue them. She would not uncover the whole truth until three years later, at the age of nineteen. That is when she enacted the most critical and difficult part of her plan: stealing the demon. That was nearly six months prior to her involvement in the events at the temple ruins.

Sarah was probably the only person in the whole galaxy that could see the barely existent shred of decency within her father. She never cared about gaining an empire. She explained to Karl how, in a misguided attempt to save her father from his own corrupt and avaricious proclivities, she devised a plan to take the demon and either destroy it or hide it far away. She summoned it using the secret books in her father's library and then trapped it using a highly volatile *Phylaca Daemonium* spell. A spell which she admits lasted much longer than she had intended. She recognized the evil her father was consumed by and hoped that removing the demon from him would have freed her father from its influence. She was wrong. She eventually discovered that only by setting this demon back into its prison-tomb could she permanently shut it away, for it had become too powerful to destroy and no other method of containment would suffice for long.

Stealing the demon meant somehow separating it from her father while he slept. She could easily get past all of his security measures. Once captured she would immediately have to leave the planet and go into hiding. The plan took a month to set up and there would only be one shot at it.

When she stole the demon and went into hiding, Icarian was furious. He still felt a tenuous connection to the demon, but its location was obscured by Sarah's spell. He had to handle this situation with great care, lest his secrets be exposed. It became a cloak and dagger chess game between father and daughter. She would delve into mysteries in one exotic location, thus alerting her father's agents, who would then seek to round her up. Only to have her slip through their fingers by the narrowest of margins, and go back into hiding. This happened again and again for five months.

Eventually Icarian pieced together her ultimate strategy by analyzing her patterns of inquiry. Once he discovered her true intent, to lock the demon back in its prison, he knew what he had to do. He knew that only the pure of heart would be allowed to enter the temple complex. He needed capable patsies to bypass the psychic tests and challenges of the prison-tomb. Sarah had left Songbird behind when she absconded with the demon. She believed Songbird would be so over-protective that she would immediately contact Icarian and report their location if she brought the automaton along.

Icarian reprogrammed the abandoned Songbird to suit his needs. Songbird's orders were to return the demon and the heiress home alive and unharmed. That girl was too rare and precious to him to allow her to be permanently harmed or killed. Icarian believed that she could be brought to heel and that she would take her place by his side as his most capable agent. Songbird's special directives were buried deep in her programming, the automaton's concern for her young ward concealed the plot for betrayal and allowed it to pass the temple's threshold with minimal disturbance. Just some minor psycho-tectonic tremors.

Sarah had gotten to the temple days in advance of Toby and Karl, but was captured by the Nightmare Queen. She used the leaking power of the gemstone to ward the monster off. Somehow the residual aura from the demon fascinated and terrified the last spider-thing. It was enough to keep the creature from devouring her or laying eggs in her skull. Her survival suit kept her alive much longer than she normally would have lasted without it. By the time the two adventurers arrived, she was very close to the limits of what the suit could handle.

Knowing his daughter was in peril inside the ruined temple complex, Icarian Phaedra gave a *masterful* performance and recruited Toby and Karl to recover her. He sent along the reprogrammed Songbird to ensure that after he got his daughter and demon back, no one would ever know about Toby, Karl, or the secrets of this temple. The temple was a prison and a tomb designed to lock away a spirit so powerful and malevolent that it couldn't be banished or destroyed. But if one could figure out the subtleties of the magical law that bound the demon to this place, one might bind it to themselves and steal it permanently. Potentially it could be permanently taken from him. So long as the temple stood this spiritual amalgam would endure.

***

The day Toby was to be transferred to the new facility, Karl said one last farewell to his best friend. Karl recited the hymn, *He Who Casts out Sorrow during the Long Night* to Toby and then pinned the *Sacred Token of Hearthkeep* onto Toby's pajama lapel like a medal of honor.

The minute you wake up, I want to know. He thought to himself as he covertly placed the Singularity Transceiver, a tiny emergency distress beacon with an infinite range, around Toby's neck with a silver chain. He tucked it under Toby's pajama top. When Toby woke up all he had to do was press the little red button on it and Karl would know that instant no matter how distant. The idea had come to him in a dream. It had cost quite a bit of Mr. Blackdagger's cash advance, but Karl felt it was well worth it.

Mr. and Mrs. Seven Hills, were dressed in somber earthen tones of the autumn season as they approached Karl with a small box in Toby Seniors' hand. "Toby wanted you to have this, Karl." said Mrs. Seven Hills as Toby Sr. handed Karl the rectangular box. Inside was *Phipps's Phlogistonickal Penknife* wrapped in a cleaning cloth.

"Oh. *Oh, guys.* You know I will keep this safe until he wakes up. He'll need this back." They nodded in the affirmative and Karl hugged them both tightly and wished them a safe journey home. They would go with Toby to the new hospital. Once everything was set up there, they would pack up Toby's things at his apartment in Malwonkee. Finally, with his belongings in tow, they would go back home to the Reservation.

"You're not going with them?" asked Sarah.

"I can't. I have a ship to catch. I've booked passage aboard Sojourn again. Captain Jones has to depart at a precise time in order to meet her other obligations. Since I'm getting a *huge* break on the cost of passage, I have be more considerate of the crew's needs.

"I just won't have time to get my stuff before my land lady, Widow Roache, puts it all out on the curb." Karl let out a hefty sigh. "I would have liked to put my things in storage or to have found a way to keep the things I have collected over the years."

"Do you have time for a coffee?" Sarah asked. "I have an offer to make."

Karl's eyes narrowed, "An offer, huh? Lately, those words rarely are followed by anything I enjoy hearing, Sarah. Coffee sounds good though."

They sat together in the hospital cafeteria and drank some barely adequate coffee together. "I know, I am sorry about my first attempt at this pitch. Let me just blurt it all out. I don't want you to lose all your stuff. So, I will pay for it all. I am going to go down to your apartment in Malwonkee, rescue what I can of yours, and then put it all safely in storage here in Corona; in my home. In one of my hundreds of spare rooms. If you give me a list of things you want shipped to you, I will take care of that too."

"Wow. Just, *wow.*" Karl set his coffee down. "I mean, I would be *really* grateful if you could! I don't know how I will pay you back."

"*Pish*! It's the least I could do, Karl. I don't have many real friends and you are a good person, Karl. I don't like it when bad things happen to you." She said sorting through the sweeteners looking for something that wouldn't cause cancer in lab rats.

"*Pish* back at you! I don't have nearly enough myself. So, I would take it as a personal kindness if you would come visit me on Sojourn as soon and as often as you can."

"I'd really like that!" Sarah smiled and crinkled her nose in a way that seemed to always be able to make Karl smile as well.

They did their best to avoid the news because every day, all day, it was about Sarah and her father. Here in the cafeteria, even with the sound muted and in the (albeit subdued) din of the families, patients, and staff here, the message came across clearly. The sun had set on her father's empire. After all was said and done, in a matter of days after Icarian Phaedra's arrest, the vast PhaedraCorp Empire had crumbled. As it fell apart, competitors tore at its carcass like vultures or jackals fighting over the largest portion of entrails. The feeding frenzy was ugly. The details scrolled across the bottom of the screen as infographics and video bites explained the news story. Sarah couldn't help but notice and when she did a little light went out of her smile.

But, Sarah was still a *mind-blowingly and incredibly* wealthy young woman whom had never truly cared about ruling over an empire anyway. She believed that she could do a lot of good with what she had left. The most difficult part was that she had no idea how to process what had happened between her and her father. Karl knew that when she was mentally adrift and in danger of being consumed by sadness it was mostly concerning her incredibly complex and painful relationship with her father.

Karl gently, nearly reflexively, nudged her index finger with his own as if to subconsciously convey his moral support and an increased gravitas in what he was about to say. "You're going through so much right now, Sarah. I really appreciate you helping me during all this mess. You really should take some time to get your head together."

"I *am* doing something for myself. I am spending more time with friends." She took his hand for the first time ever and squeezed. Her smile returned, restored to full radiance, and in that instant seemed very much like fireworks on a warm summer night and his heart nearly skipped a beat. He dismissed the strange and almost pleasantly ticklish feeling and simply smiled back bashfully as he drank his cooling coffee. They held hands quietly until it was time to leave for Sojourn.

***

Sarah gave him a long hug goodbye before leaving him at the spaceport. She stayed and watched him until he disappeared into the mass of travelers coming and going from all points in the galaxy.

When Karl first set foot back onto Sojourn, he felt the sting of Toby's absence. Captain Jones and Mr. Tor were there to greet him just inside the airlock. "Welcome aboard Karl." Said the captain.

"Hello, Captain. Good afternoon, Mr. Tor." Karl extended his hand. Tor was the impenetrable stone wall of stoicism he always was, but managed to raise an eyebrow at Karl's vigorous and cheerful attempt at a hand shake.

She elbowed her friend as a gentle reminder to be polite and he acquiesced. Mr. Tor quickly shook Karl's hand and swiftly pulled his hand back.

Captain Jones shook her head at Mr. Tor and then gave Karl a hug. "I am so sorry to hear about what happened to your friend, Karl. You two were very brave."

Karl's smile waivered nearly imperceptibly as the heart ache he felt over his friend made its way to the surface, but he quickly recovered. "Toby will be all right. He's just taking a long rest." He thought about what his mother had said in the dream he had before waking up in the hospital. "Everything will be okay."

"Your letter stated that you were interested in joining us for an indefinite stay?" Captain Jones inquired.

"Yes. I hope that won't be a problem." Karl asked.

"Not at all. We've found you a bunk in the crew quarters. It's not as luxurious as your previous accommodations, but you will have privacy rumbles and shifts from beneath. A slender figure slowly emerges from the mass of collapsed stone into the punishing winds of a snow storm. The nymph-like clockwork figure effortlessly heaves a huge stone boulder out of her way and gazes upward at the angry skies pouring down snow. A blazing blood red gemstone flares brilliantly like a dying star imbedded in the center of her forehead. It gives silent warning to the winter night that something new and terrible has been born from the ruins. Without a word, consumed with vengeance, she begins her long trek down the mountain.

End

Coming soon,

Sojourn: the Continuing Adventures of Karl.

18390211R00069

Made in the USA
San Bernardino, CA
12 January 2015